A BOOK OF BOSH

Edward Lear was very fond of bosh; fond of the word and fond of what it stood for: 'stuff and nonsense'. He once wrote to a friend that he would like to get the prime minister to appoint him Grand Peripatetic Ass and Bosh-producing Luminary, and readers of this book will find that he even invented a word which meant something like 'bosh multiplied by ten'.

In putting together these Learical Lyrics and Puffles of Prose (a book title which Lear himself thought of using) Brian Alderson has tried to show something of the range of bosh that Edward Lear actually produced. As well as the limericks and nonsense songs that almost everyone knows about, there are less familiar poems, rhymes and drawings, together with a few 'eggstrax' from his letters and a dictionary of his 'wurbl inwentions'. The artist's gloomy experiences among mucilaginous monks in Athos, and burst water-pipes at Walton-on-Thames are recounted with the same strange blend of exhilaration and sensitivity that he brought to the conversation between Mr Daddy Long-legs and Mr Floppy Fly, or the adventures of agèd Uncle Arly – clipfombious to the last degree.

Lyrics and Prose of

EDWARD LEAR

A BOOK OF
BOSH

CHOSEN BY
BRIAN ALDERSON

PUFFIN BOOKS

PUFFIN BOOKS

Published by the Penguin Group
Penguin Books Ltd, 27 Wrights Lane, London W8 5TZ, England
Penguin Books USA Inc., 375 Hudson Street, New York, New York 10014, USA
Penguin Books Australia Ltd, Ringwood, Victoria, Australia
Penguin Books Canada Ltd, 2801 John Street, Markham, Ontario, Canada L3R 1B4
Penguin Books (NZ) Ltd, 182–190 Wairau Road, Auckland 10, New Zealand

Penguin Books Ltd, Registered Offices: Harmondsworth, Middlesex, England

First published 1975
Reissued 1992
1 3 5 7 9 10 8 6 4 2

Printed in England by Clays Ltd, St Ives plc
Set in Monotype Modern Extended

CONTENTS

Preface 7

I Derry down Derry 15

II Birds and Beasticles 59

III Paraphernalia 73

IV Mrs Jaypher's Wisdom 89

V Abstemious Asses, Zealous Zebras and others 101

VI Two Stories 135

VII An Episode of Noses 155

VIII Two Tales of the Jumblies 165

IX The Lonely Shore 175

X Some Incidents in the Life of Edward Lear 187

Receipt for Sauces 214

Acknowledgements 216

FOR KAYE

with love and admiration

from

Brian

and from

the ghost of Uncle Arly

(though his shoes are far too tight)

*

Ploffskin, Pluffskin, Pelican jay
Pomskizillious Puffin Kaye
Plumpskin, Ploshkin, Pelican jill,
We think so then, and we thought so still.

PREFACE

WHATEVER happened to the Earl of Derby's grandchildren?

Instead of dutifully attending upon their Grandpapa after dinner, they disappeared . . . and were discovered in the steward's quarters talking to a young man who had come up from London to draw pictures of the animals in the Earl's menagerie.

And whatever was Queen Victoria's drawing-master up to?

He would keep tittupping in front of the fireplace (where only Royalty should stand). Then later, when he saw the Queen's collection of miniatures he cried out, 'Oh! where *did* you get all these beautiful things?' as if the Queen had just been out shopping, and the Queen replied: 'I inherited them, Mr Lear.'

Kindly, innocent, fussed-and-bothered Edward Lear! He passed through proud and respectable Victorian society as though he were walking in a dream. Knowing, and befriended by, some of the greatest men of his age, he never quite stood with them, but always a little to one side – something of a poor relation at their enormous dinner-parties, a landscape-painter who may have depended on them to commission his work, but who owed none of them a penny for his genius.

Those grandchildren of the Earl of Derby knew what they were about. In a world that did not have too much to offer them beyond 'Conversations with Mama on the Conduct of a Virtuous Life', they had found unexpected treasure: a curious, comical person who sang songs and pulled faces and cracked jokes – and then would take out his sketch-pad and draw pictures for his own rhymes:

> There was an Old Man with a beard,
> Who said, 'It is just as I feared! –
> Two Owls and a Hen, four Larks and a Wren,
> Have all built their nests in my beard!'

and there was the drawing (at the top of the next page) to prove it with the Old Man looking faintly like young Mr Lear.

Some people have said that Edward Lear invented this sort of rhyme (which, for no known reason, is called a Limerick). As it happens, though, he did not, for he admitted to getting the idea from a little book called *The Anecdotes and Adventures of Fifteen Gentlemen*, and he even made sketches for one of its rhymes:

> There was a sick Man of Tobago
> Lived long on Rice Gruel and Sago
> Till one day to his bliss, the physician said this –
> 'To roast leg of mutton you may go'.

But even though he didn't invent Limericks, he was certainly the reason for their becoming so popular. He revelled in the opportunity that they gave him to say nonsensical things, and although we nowadays think of Limericks more as jokes – like the modern rhyme,

There was a young lady of Ryde,
Who ate a green apple and died,
But the apple fermented inside the lamented
And made cider inside 'er inside.

no writer has ever equalled Lear's skill at combining preposterous events with similarly preposterous drawings.

As in the earlier years of his career, so later, Edward Lear was always ready to respond to the quick pleasure that children took in his 'nonsenses'. Stricter grown-ups, it is true, might prove to be ojous or scroobious (discover these words on pages 209 and 210) but children never worried about laughing too much and Lear fed their laughter – sometimes with more Limericks, sometimes with comic tales or ballads. And where the schoolbooks served up learning as solemnly as possible, Mr Lear made nonsense of the alphabet, and even of botany.

Despite the fact that he was always eager to give enjoyment to others, Edward Lear himself had a hard and rather melancholy life. It began all wrong, with a childhood compounded of loneliness, neglect and illness, and the wonder is not just that he became, in his own way, a great man, but that he kept faith with laughter, even when things were at their most desperate.

What facts we know of his early life suggest little promise for his future at all. Born on 12 May 1812, he was the twentieth child in a family that was finally to number twenty-one, and it seems clear that his parents had little affection for him. To make matters worse, soon after his birth, his father, who was a fairly well-to-do man of business in the City of London, ran into serious financial troubles and what family life the boy knew disintegrated almost completely.

For much of his early life Edward Lear was more dependent

9

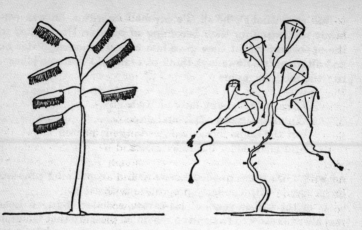

Two Botanical Drawings by Edward Lear

The Clothes-Brush Tree This most useful natural production does not produce many clothesbrushes, which accounts for those objects being expensive. The omsquombious nature of this extraordinary vegetable it is of course unnecessary to be diffuse upon.

The Kite Tree is a fearful and astonishing vegetable when all the kites are agitated by a tremendous wind, and endeavour to escape from their strings. The tree does not not appear to be of any particular use to society, but would be frequented by small boys if they knew where it grew.

upon his sister, Ann, than anyone else, and, since she was twenty-two years older than he was she became a mother to him in all but fact. It was she who taught him his early lessons, she who encouraged his love of drawing, and she who looked after him during his numerous illnesses. For to add to his other troubles he was a child of delicate health, very short-sighted and, worst of all, subject to attacks of epilepsy. Lear was a victim of these attacks from the age of five or six onwards and, although they became less frequent as he grew older, they were always a source of great worry and unhappiness.

When the time came for him to seek a living of his own, he was drawn to nothing so much as the life of what he later pleased

10

to call 'a nartist'. For all that he had no formal training, he achieved a mastery in the portrayal of birds and animals (and it was indeed the success of his work in illustrating books on parrots, tortoises and exotic birds that caused the Earl of Derby to summon him to draw pictures of his menagerie). However, the close, detailed work that was required of a painter of animals eventually became too much of a strain for his eyes and in 1837 he decided to turn to landscape-painting; it was in this field of art that he was to earn his living for the rest of his life.

Drawing animals in Northern England had had a damaging effect on more than just his eyesight though; it had also brought on more frequent bouts of bronchitis and asthma, the ailments of his childhood. Consequently, along with his decision to become a landscape-painter, there followed a realization that much of his work should be done in a warmer, drier climate than that of England, and from 1837 he began the life of a traveller.

For more than thirty years after this date he had no real home, and spent his time moving from place to place, mostly in the lands that border the Mediterranean. He became the prototype of his own 'Uncle Arly', but instead of subsisting:

> ... by teaching children spelling, –
> Or at times by merely yelling, –
> Or at intervals by selling
> Propter's Nicodemus Pills,

he worked at his landscapes, which he might prepare to the order of wealthy patrons, or exhibit for sale in galleries, or use as the basis for the illustration of travel books. It was the publication in 1846 of his *Illustrated Excursions in Italy* that caught the attention of Queen Victoria and led her to appoint him to give her a course of twelve drawing lessons (and she recorded in her diary that 'he teaches remarkably well').

In all the time of travelling and in his last years up to his death in 1888 when he was living in his own house at San Remo, on the Italian Riviera, Edward Lear showed a great genius for human sympathy. He never married, never had children of his own, but throughout what he called his 'hurried, boshy life' he made (and kept) innumerable friends and, at a time when manners were often strict and formal, he had a natural and easygoing way which delighted children. Like so many Victorians he was possessed of enormous energy (or, as he preferred to put it 'N.R.G.') and the Limericks, verses and alphabets that he would recite to children were only a small part of a creative life that produced hundreds upon hundreds of sketches, drawings and paintings and a huge quantity of other writing, from published books about his travels in Italy, Greece and Albania, to a multitude of manuscript diaries and letters.

In all but his most formal *worx* nonsense is never very far away. It may occur in descriptions, like his fierce account of a a visit to the monasteries of Mount Athos (p. 193), or in drawings like this one of himself, his beloved cat Foss, and some friendly birds:

or in some ridiculous play on words. He delighted in puns and riddles ('What would Neptune say if they deprived him of the sea?' – 'I haven't a/n otion!') and he was for ever inventing or adapting words – sometimes ('squondangerlous', 'gromfibberous') because he enjoyed the noise they made, and sometimes as a kind of defence, a refusal to show that he was lonely, or frightened, or that he felt himself out of his depth in high Victorian society:

> I was disgusted at being aperiently so rude to Lady Waldegrave – but I was not well from the East winds, and so completely uncertain whether I had any voice or not, that I thought it better not to sing, than to go to the piano and be obliged to quit it. I felt like a cow who has swallowed a glass bottle – or a boiled weasel – and should probably have made a noise like a dyspeptic mouse in a fit. [From a letter, Sept. 1863].

You may find as you read this selection of Edward Lear's writing that there is more to it than just 'nonsense'; there is an undertow of fear and sadness. Not all the Limericks, for instance, are entirely easygoing:

> There was an Old Man with a gong,
> Who bumped at it all the day long;
> But they called out, 'O law! you're a horrid old bore!'
> So they smashed that Old Man with a gong.

and in the nonsense songs terrible things occur: the Yonghy-Bonghy-Bò must part for ever from the Lady Jingly Jones, and the Dong is left alone 'on the cruel shore'; the Two Old Bachelors disappear into oblivion and Mr Discobbolos brings about a cataclysmic horror. The sound of loss, deprivation and destruction is sharper and sometimes more heroic for being found within the nonsense – particularly when it is such sweetly written nonsense as Mr Lear's. There is a strange tension between the music of his poetry, its rhymes and rhythms, and its sadness. Whoever else could have made two lines like the following (written in a letter to a friend) at once both funny and hopeless:

> But never more. O! never we –
> Shall meet to eggs and toast and T!

The selection of Edward Lear's *worx* that has been put together here has been drawn from a variety of what he called his 'volumes of stuff' – and I have been careful to include as many of his drawings as possible. (Funnily enough, people do not always realize that Lear was an artist by profession and that many of his 'serious' drawings of animals and landscapes are of exceptional quality: 'He can't draw properly', they say; or 'It's too scribbly', without appreciating that he knew just how to get the effects that he wanted and that too much 'realism' would spoil the comedy.)

The present book starts with a plentiful supply of Limericks and then goes on to offer a jumble of nonsense-songs, stories, alphabets and the like – some of which are in all the books of Lear and some of which are much less well-known. These writings may not look very jumblish, because they have been neatly divided up into 'chapters', but they have the chief quality of any jumble which is that it doesn't much matter where you begin looking at it, or what direction you go in once you've started. If anyone wants to know where everything came from and whom I have to thank for it then there are some lists on pages 215-17.

Just before these, in the final 'chapter' of the book, you will find a rather peculiar collection of *eggstrax* from Edward Lear's letters, together with one or two other oddities. These have been assembled partly as an excuse for including some more of his drawings, and partly because they help to show how far his 'nonsense' was present in everything he did. Despite pessimistic Germans and mucilaginous monks a kind of cheerfulness would keep breaking in – it did so then, and it does so still, and we very much hope that you will enjoy it.

BRIAN ALDERSON

I
DERRY DOWN DERRY

There was an Old Derry down Derry,
Who loved to see little folks merry;
So he made them a book, and with laughter they shook
At the fun of that Derry down Derry.

There was an old person of Brigg,
Who purchased no end of a wig;
So that only his nose, and the end of his toes,
Could be seen when he walked about Brigg.

There was a young lady in blue,
Who said, 'Is it you? Is it you?'
When they said, 'Yes, it is,' – She replied only, 'Whizz!'
That ungracious young lady in blue.

There was an old person of Wick,
Who said, 'Tick-a-Tick, Tick-a-Tick;
Chickabee, Chickabaw,' And he said nothing more,
That laconic old person of Wick.

There was an old person of Harrow,
Who bought a mahogany barrow,
For he said to his wife, 'You're the joy of my life!
And I'll wheel you all day in this barrow!'

There was an old man of Dumbree,
Who taught little owls to drink tea;
For he said, 'To eat mice, is not proper or nice,'
That amiable man of Dumbree.

There was a Young Lady whose eyes,
Were unique as to colour and size;
When she opened them wide, people all turned aside,
And started away in surprise.

There was an Old Man who supposed,
That the street door was partially closed;
But some very large rats, ate his coats and his hats,
While that futile old gentleman dozed.

There was an Old Person of Buda,
Whose conduct grew ruder and ruder;
Till at last, with a hammer, they silenced his clamour,
By smashing that Person of Buda.

There was an old person of Bradley,
Who sang all so loudly and sadly;
With a poker and tongs he beat time to his songs,
That melodious old person of Bradley.

There was an old person of Newry,
Whose manners were tinctured with fury;
He tore all the rugs, and broke all the jugs
Within twenty miles' distance of Newry.

There was an Old Man with an owl,
Who continued to bother and howl;
He sate on a rail, and imbibed bitter ale,
Which refreshed that Old Man and his owl.

There was a Young Lady whose chin,
Resembled the point of a pin;
So she had it made sharp, and purchased a harp,
And played several tunes with her chin.

There was an Old Man of Cape Horn,
Who wished he had never been born;
So he sat on a chair, till he died of despair,
That dolorous Man of Cape Horn.

There was an old man of Kildare,
Who climbed into a very high chair;
When he said, – 'Here I stays, till the end of my days',
That immovable man of Kildare.

There was an Old Man of the Hague,
Whose ideas were excessively vague;
He built a balloon, to examine the moon,
That deluded Old Man of the Hague.

There was an Old Man who said, 'Hush!
I perceive a young bird in this bush!'
When they said – 'Is it small?' He replied – 'Not at all!
It is four times as big as the bush!'

There was an old man, who when little
Fell casually into a kettle;
But, growing too stout, he could never get out,
So he passed all his life in that kettle.

There was an old man of Spithead,
Who opened the window, and said, –
'Fil-jomble, fil-jumble, fil-rumble-come-tumble!'
That doubtful old man of Spithead.

There was an old man of New York,
Who murdered himself with a fork;
But nobody cried, though he very soon died,
For that silly old man of New York.

There was an old man who screamed out
Whenever they knocked him about;
So they took off his boots, and fed him with fruits,
And continued to knock him about.

There was an old man on the Border,
Who lived in the utmost disorder;
He danced with the cat, and made tea in his hat,
Which vexed all the folks on the Border.

There was an Old Man of Whitehaven,
Who danced a quadrille with a Raven;
But they said – 'It's absurd, to encourage this bird!'
So they smashed that Old Man of Whitehaven.

There was an old person of Bromley,
Whose ways were not cheerful or comely;
He sate in the dust, eating spiders and crust,
That unpleasing old person of Bromley.

There was an old person of Pinner,
As thin as a lath, if not thinner;
They dressed him in white, and roll'd him up tight,
That elastic old person of Pinner.

There was an Old Man with a poker,
Who painted his face with red oker;
When they said, 'You're a Guy!' he made no reply,
But knocked them all down with his poker.

There was an old man of Dunrose;
A parrot seized hold of his nose.
When he grew melancholy, they said, 'His name's Polly,'
Which soothed that old man of Dunrose.

There was an old person of Sestri,
Who sate himself down in the vestry,
When they said 'You are wrong!' – he merely said 'Bong!'
That repulsive old person of Sestri.

There was an old man in a tree,
Whose whiskers were lovely to see;
But the birds of the air, pluck'd them perfectly bare,
To make themselves nests in that tree.

There was an Old Man of the Nile,
Who sharpened his nails with a file;
Till he cut off his thumbs, and said calmly, 'This comes –
Of sharpening one's nails with a file!'

There was an old person of Jodd,
Whose ways were perplexing and odd;
She purchased a whistle, and sate on a thistle,
And squeaked to the people of Jodd.

There was an old person of Stroud,
Who was horribly jammed in a crowd;
Some she slew with a kick, some she scrunched with a stick,
That impulsive old person of Stroud.

There was an old man of Hong Kong,
Who never did anything wrong;
He lay on his back, with his head in a sack,
That innocuous old man of Hong Kong.

There was an old person of Grange,
Whose manners were scroobious and strange;
He sailed to St Blubb, in a waterproof tub,
That aquatic old person of Grange.

There was an Old Man of Calcutta,
Who perpetually ate bread and butter;
Till a great bit of muffin, on which he was stuffing,
Choked that horrid old man of Calcutta.

There was an old person of Ware,
Who rode on the back of a bear:
When they ask'd, – 'Does it trot?' – he said 'Certainly not!
He's a Moppsikon Floppsikon bear!'

There was an Old Man on some rocks,
Who shut his wife up in a box,
When she said, 'Let me out,' he exclaimed, 'Without doubt,
You will pass all your life in that box.'

There was an old person of Putney,
Whose food was roast spiders and chutney,
Which he took with his tea, within sight of the sea,
That romantic old person of Putney.

There was an Old Person whose habits,
Induced him to feed upon Rabbits;
When he'd eaten eighteen, he turned perfectly green,
Upon which he relinquished those habits.

There was an Old Man in a boat,
Who said, 'I'm afloat! I'm afloat!'
When they said, 'No! you ain't!' he was ready to faint,
That unhappy Old Man in a boat.

There was an Old Man who said, 'Well!
Will *nobody* answer this bell?
I have pulled day and night, till my hair has grown white,
But nobody answers this bell!'

There was an Old Man with a gong,
Who bumped at it all the day long;
But they called out, 'O law! you're a horrid old bore!'
So they smashed that Old Man with a gong.

II
BIRDS AND BEASTICLES

I asked the girl here (having a friend to
dine, and wishing to have the wine cool)
for some ice. But she thought I said, I want
some *mice!* and was seized with great fear
forthwith.

THE DADDY LONG-LEGS AND THE FLY

I

Once Mr Daddy Long-legs,
　　Dressed in brown and gray,
Walked about upon the sands
　　Upon a summer's day;
And there among the pebbles,
　　When the wind was rather cold,
He met with Mr Floppy Fly,
　　All dressed in blue and gold.
And as it was too soon to dine,
They drank some Periwinkle-wine,
And played an hour or two, or more,
At battlecock and shuttledore.

II

Said Mr Daddy Long-legs
　　To Mr Floppy Fly,
'Why do you never come to court?
　　I wish you'd tell me why.
All gold and shine, in dress so fine,
　　You'd quite delight the court.

Why do you never go at all?
    I really think you *ought!*
And if you went, you'd see such sights!
Such rugs! and jugs! and candle-lights!
And more than all, the King and Queen,
One in red, and one in green!'

III

'O Mr Daddy Long-legs,'
    Said Mr Floppy Fly,
'It's true I never go to court,
    And I will tell you why.
If I had six long legs like yours,
    At once I'd go to court!
But oh! I can't, because *my* legs
    Are so extremely short.
And I'm afraid the King and Queen
(One in red, and one in green)
Would say aloud, "You are not fit,
You Fly, to come to court a bit!" '

IV

'O Mr Daddy Long-legs,'
    Said Mr Floppy Fly,
'I wish you'd sing one little song!
    One mumbian melody!
You used to sing so awful well
    In former days gone by,
But now you never sing at all;
    I wish you'd tell me why:
For if you would, the silvery sound
Would please the shrimps and cockles round,
And all the crabs would gladly come
To hear you sing, "Ah, Hum di Hum"!'

V

Said Mr Daddy Long-legs,
  'I can never sing again!
And if you wish, I'll tell you why,
  Although it gives me pain.
For years I cannot hum a bit,
  Or sing the smallest song;
And this the dreadful reason is,
  My legs are grown too long!
My six long legs, all here and there,
Oppress my bosom with despair;
And if I stand, or lie, or sit,
I cannot sing one single bit!'

VI

So Mr Daddy Long-legs
  And Mr Floppy Fly
Sat down in silence by the sea,
  And gazed upon the sky.
They said, 'This is a dreadful thing!
The world has all gone wrong,
Since one has legs too short by half,
  The other much too long!
One never more can go to court,
Because his legs have grown too short;
The other cannot sing a song,
Because his legs have grown too long!'

VII

Then Mr Daddy Long-legs
  And Mr Floppy Fly
Rushed downward to the foamy sea
  With one sponge-taneous cry;
And there they found a little boat,
  Whose sails were pink and gray;

And off they sailed among the waves,
   Far, and far away.
They sailed across the silent main,
And reached the great Gromboolian plain;
And there they play for evermore
At battlecock and shuttledoor.

THE OWL AND THE PUSSY-CAT

I

The Owl and the Pussy-cat went to sea   *A*
  In a beautiful pea-green boat,   *B*
They took some honey, and plenty of money,   *C*
  Wrapped up in a five-pound note.   *B*
The Owl looked up to the stars above,   *D*
  And sang to a small guitar,   *E*
'O lovely Pussy! O Pussy, my love,   *D*
  What a beautiful Pussy you are,   *E*
    You are,   *E*
    You are!   *E*
  What a beautiful Pussy you are!'   *E*

Ballad stanza

II

Pussy said to the Owl, 'You elegant fowl!   *A*
  How charmingly sweet you sing!   *B*
O let us be married! too long we have tarried: *C*
  But what shall we do for a ring?'   *B*
They sailed away, for a year and a day,   *Internal rhyme*
  To the land where the Bong-tree grows
And there in a wood a Piggy-wig stood
  With a ring at the end of his nose,
    His nose,
    His nose,
  With a ring at the end of his nose.

III

'Dear Pig, are you willing to sell for one shilling
   Your ring?' Said the Piggy, 'I will.'
So they took it away, and were married next day
   By the Turkey who lives on the hill.
They dined on mince, and slices of quince,
   Which they ate with a runcible spoon;
And hand in hand, on the edge of the sand,
   They danced by the light of the moon,
     The moon,
     The moon,
They danced by the light of the moon.

THE PELICAN CHORUS

King and Queen of the Pelicans we;
No other Birds so grand we see!
None but we have feet like fins!
With lovely leathery throats and chins!
  Ploffskin, Pluffskin, Pelican jee!
  We think no Birds so happy as we!
  Plumpskin, Ploshkin, Pelican jill!
  We think so then, and we thought so still!

We live on the Nile. The Nile we love.
By night we sleep on the cliffs above;
By day we fish, and at eve we stand
On long bare islands of yellow sand.
And when the sun sinks slowly down
And the great rock walls grow dark and brown,
Where the purple river rolls fast and dim
And the Ivory Ibis starlike skim,
Wing to wing we dance around, –
Stamping our feet with a flumpy sound, –
Opening our mouths as Pelicans ought,
And this is the song we nightly snort; –

Ploffskin, Pluffskin, Pelican jee, –
We think no Birds so happy as we!
Plumpskin, Ploshkin, Pelican jill, –
We think so then, and we thought so still.

Last year came out our Daughter, Dell;
And all the Birds received her well.
To do her honour, a feast we made
For every bird that can swim or wade.
Herons and Gulls, and Cormorants black,
Cranes, and Flamingoes with scarlet back,
Plovers and Storks, and Geese in clouds,
Swans and Dilberry Ducks in crowds.
Thousands of Birds in wondrous flight!
They ate and drank and danced all night,
And echoing back from the rocks you heard
Multitude-echoes from Bird and Bird, –
   Ploffskin, Pluffskin, Pelican jee,
   We think no Birds so happy as we!
   Plumpskin, Ploshkin, Pelican jill,
   We think so then, and we thought so still!

Yes, they came; and among the rest,
The King of the Cranes all grandly dressed.
Such a lovely tail! Its feathers float
Between the ends of his blue dress-coat;
With pea-green trowsers all so neat,
And a delicate frill to hide his feet, –
(For though no one speaks of it, every one knows,
He has got no webs between his toes!)

As soon as he saw our Daughter Dell,
In violent love that Crane King fell, –
On seeing her waddling form so fair,
With a wreath of shrimps in her short white hair.
And before the end of the next long day,
Our Dell had given her heart away;

For the King of the Cranes had won that heart,
With a Crocodile's egg and a large fish-tart.
She vowed to marry the King of the Cranes,
Leaving the Nile for stranger plains;
And away they flew in a gathering crowd
Of endless birds in a lengthening cloud.
   Ploffskin, Pluffskin, Pelican jee,
    We think no Birds so happy as we!
    Plumpskin, Ploshkin, Pelican jill,
    We think so then, and we thought so still!

And far away in the twilight sky,
We heard them singing a lessening cry, —
Farther and farther till out of sight,
And we stood alone in the silent night!
Often since, in the nights of June,
We sit on the sand and watch the moon; —
She has gone to the great Gromboolian plain,
And we probably never shall meet again!
Oft, in the long still nights of June,
We sit on the rocks and watch the moon; —
— She dwells by the streams of the Chankly Bore,
And we probably never shall see her more.
   Ploffskin, Pluffskin, Pelican jee,
    We think no Birds so happy as we!
    Plumpskin, Ploshkin, Pelican jill,
    We think so then, and we thought so still!

THE DUCK AND THE KANGAROO

I

Said the Duck to the Kangaroo,
  'Good gracious! how you hop!
Over the fields and the water too,
  As if you never would stop!
My life is a bore in this nasty pond,
And I long to go out in the world beyond!
  I wish I could hop like you!'
  Said the Duck to the Kangaroo.

II

'Please give me a ride on your back!'
  Said the Duck to the Kangaroo.
'I would sit quite still, and say nothing but "Quack",
  The whole of the long day through!
And we'd go to the Dee, and the Jelly Bo Lee,
Over the land, and over the sea; —
  Please take me a ride! O do!'
  Said the Duck to the Kangaroo.

III

Said the Kangaroo to the Duck,
  'This requires some little reflection;
Perhaps on the whole it might bring me luck,
  And there seems but one objection,
Which is, if you'll let me speak so bold,
Your feet are unpleasantly wet and cold,
And would probably give me the roo-
  Matiz!' said the Kangaroo.

Said the Duck, 'As I sat on the rocks,
   I have thought over that completely,
And I bought four pairs of worsted socks
   Which fit my web-feet neatly.
And to keep out the cold I've bought a cloak,
And every day a cigar I'll smoke,
    All to follow my own dear true
    Love of a Kangaroo!'

Said the Kangaroo, 'I'm ready!
   All in the moonlight pale;
But to balance me well, dear Duck, sit steady!
   And quite at the end of my tail!'
So away they went with a hop and a bound,
And they hopped the whole world three times round;
    And who so happy, – O who,
    As the Duck and the Kangaroo?

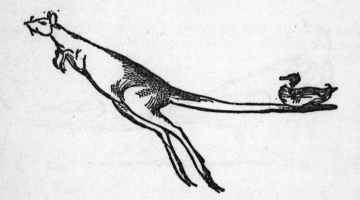

III
PARAPHERNALIA

1. ye traveller
2. ye Railewaie rugge
3. ye author his vestmentes
4. his hatteboxe
5. ye cheste of draweres
6. ye chaire
7. ye large cheste
8. ye washingtable
9. ye drying table
10. ye traveller his bootes
11. ye sparkling looking glasse
12. ye table
13. ye tinne tubbe
14. ye china tub
15. ye matting rolled uppe
16. ye quadrangular pincushione
17. ye jugge
18. ye flaskes of gunnepowder
19. ye picklejarres
20. ye beautiful chaire made of wickerworke
21. ye peaceful cherubbes that appeared to ye author when he fell asleepe.

Drawing of ye poppular author & traveller in Albania & Calabria, keepinge his feete warme.

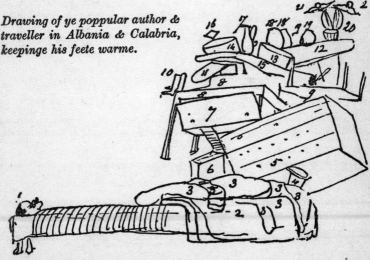

THE TABLE AND
THE CHAIR

I

Said the Table to the Chair,
'You can hardly be aware,
'How I suffer from the heat,
'And from chilblains on my feet!
'If we took a little walk,
'We might have a little talk!
'Pray let us take the air!'
Said the Table to the Chair.

II

Said the Chair unto the Table,
'Now you *know* we are not able!
'How foolishly you talk,
'When you know we *cannot* walk!'
Said the Table, with a sigh,
'It can do no harm to try,
'I've as many legs as you,
'Why can't we walk on two?'

So they both went slowly down,
And walked about the town
With a cheerful bumpy sound,
As they toddled round and round.
And everybody cried,
As they hastened to their side,
'See! the Table and the Chair
'Have come out to take the air!'

IV

But in going down an alley,
To a castle in a valley,
They completely lost their way,
And wandered all the day,

Till, to see them safely back,
They paid a Ducky-quack,
And a Beetle, and a Mouse,
Who took them to their house.

V

Then they whispered to each other,
'O delightful little brother!
'What a lovely walk we've taken!
'Let us dine on Beans and Bacon!'

So the Ducky, and the leetle
Browny-Mousy and the Beetle
Dined, and danced upon their heads
Till they toddled to their beds.

THE BROOM, THE SHOVEL,
THE POKER AND THE TONGS

I

The Broom and the Shovel, the Poker and Tongs,
  They all took a drive in the Park,
And they each sang a song, Ding-a-dong, Ding-a-dong,
  Before they went back in the dark.
Mr Poker he sate quite upright in the coach,
  Mr Tongs made a clatter and clash,
Miss Shovel was dressed all in black (with a brooch),
  Mrs Broom was in blue (with a sash).
    Ding-a-dong! Ding-a-dong!
    And they all sang a song!

II

'O Shovely so lovely!' the Poker he sang,
  'You have perfectly conquered my heart!
'Ding-a-dong! Ding-a-dong! If you're pleased with my song,
  'I will feed you with cold apple tart!
'When you scrape up the coals with a delicate sound,
  'You enrapture my life with delight!
'Your nose is so shiny! your head is so round!
  'And your shape is so slender and bright!
    'Ding-a-dong! Ding-a-dong!
    'Ain't you pleased with my song?'

'Alas! Mrs Broom!' sighed the Tongs in his song,
  'O is it because I'm so thin,
'And my legs are so long – Ding-a-dong! Ding-a-dong!
  'That you don't care about me a pin?
'Ah! fairest of creatures, when sweeping the room,
  'Ah! why don't you heed my complaint!
'Must you needs be so cruel, you beautiful Broom,
   'Because you are covered with paint?
    'Ding-a-dong! Ding-a-dong!
    'You are certainly wrong!'

IV

Mrs Broom and Miss Shovel together they sang,
  'What nonsense you're singing to-day!'
Said the Shovel, 'I'll certainly hit you a bang!'
  Said the Broom, 'And I'll sweep you away!'
So the Coachman drove homeward as fast as he could,
  Perceiving their anger with pain;
But they put on the kettle, and little by little,
  They all became happy again.
    Ding-a-dong! Ding-a-dong!
    There's an end of my song!

THE NUTCRACKERS AND THE
SUGAR-TONGS

I

The Nutcrackers sate by a plate on the table,
  The Sugar-tongs sate by a plate at his side;
And the Nutcrackers said, 'Don't you wish we were able
  'Along the blue hills and green meadows to ride?
'Must we drag on this stupid existence for ever,
  'So idle and weary, so full of remorse, –
'While every one else takes his pleasure, and never
  'Seems happy unless he is riding a horse?

II

'Don't you think we could ride without being instructed?
  'Without any saddle, or bridle, or spur?
'Our legs are so long, and so aptly constructed,
  'I'm sure that an accident could not occur.
'Let us all of a sudden hop down from the table,
  'And hustle downstairs, and each jump on a horse!
'Shall we try? Shall we go? Do you think we are able?'
  The Sugar-tongs answered distinctly, 'Of course!'

III

So down the long staircase they hopped in a minute,
  The Sugar-tongs snapped, and the Crackers said 'crack!'
The stable was open, the horses were in it;
  Each took out a pony, and jumped on his back.

The Cat in a fright scrambled out of the doorway,
  The Mice tumbled out of a bundle of hay,
The brown and white Rats, and the black ones from Norway,
  Screamed out, 'They are taking the horses away!'

IV

The whole of the household was filled with amazement,
  The Cups and the Saucers danced madly about,
The Plates and the Dishes looked out of the casement,
  The Saltcellar stood on his head with a shout,
The Spoons with a clatter looked out of the lattice,
  The Mustard-pot climbed up the Gooseberry Pies,
The Soup-ladle peeped through a heap of Veal Patties,
  And squeaked with a ladle-like scream of surprise.

V

The Frying-pan said, 'It's an awful delusion!'
  The Tea-kettle hissed and grew black in the face;
And they all rushed downstairs in the wildest confusion,
  To see the great Nutcracker-Sugar-tong race.
And out of the stable, with screamings and laughter,
  (Their ponies were cream-coloured, speckled with brown,)
The Nutcrackers first, and the Sugar-tongs after,
  Rode all round the yard, and then all round the town.

VI

They rode through the street, and they rode by the station,
  They galloped away to the beautiful shore;
In silence they rode, and 'made no observation',
  Save this: 'We will never go back any more!'
And still you might hear, till they rode out of hearing,
  The Sugar-tongs snap, and the Crackers say 'crack!'
Till far in the distance their forms disappearing,
  They faded away. – And they never came back!

A MIDWINTER DISASTER

From a letter to Emily Tennyson (wife of the Poet Laureate), dated 30 December 1860

'Lo! as I began to write this afternoon, horrible borrible squash-fibolious meligoposhquilous sounds were heard & ever increasingly, like 5000 whales in hysterics.

 Then – huming screams & shouts. – Then stamping; roaring; – rushing; – bouncing; – booming; – by-go-bustling; –
... O! ...

the great cistern, along of the sudden thaw – had bust all the pipes – which spouted forth arm-broad torrents of water like fire from cannons.'

MR AND MRS DISCOBBOLOS

spiders?

I

Mr and Mrs Discobbolos
   Climbed to the top of a wall.
 And they sate to watch the sunset sky
 And to hear the Nupiter Piffkin cry
  And the Biscuit Buffalo call.
They took up a roll and some Camomile tea,
And both were as happy as happy could be –
   Till Mrs Discobbolos said, –
   'Oh! W! X! Y! Z!
   'It has just come into my head –
'Suppose we should happen to fall! ! ! ! !
    'Darling Mr Discobbolos!

II

'Suppose we should fall down flumpetty
   'Just like pieces of stone!
 'On to the thorns, – or into the moat!
 'What would become of your new green coat
  'And might you not break a bone?
'It never occurred to me before –
'That perhaps we shall never go down any more!'
   And Mrs Discobbolos said –
   'Oh! W! X! Y! Z!
   'What put it into your head
'To climb up this wall? – my own
    'Darling Mr Discobbolos?'

Mr Discobbolos answered, –
    'At first it gave me pain, –
   'And I felt my ears turn perfectly pink
   'When your exclamation made me think
    'We might never get down again!
'But now I believe it is wiser far
'To remain for ever just where we are.' –
    And Mr Discobbolos said,
      'Oh! W! X! Y! Z!
      'It has just come into my head –
'– We shall never go down again –
      'Dearest Mrs Discobbolos!'

So Mr and Mrs Discobbolos
    Stood up, and began to sing,
   'Far away from hurry and strife
'Here we will pass the rest of life,
    'Ding a dong, ding dong, ding!
'We want no knives nor forks nor chairs,
'No tables nor carpets nor household cares,
    'From worry of life we've fled –
      'Oh! W! X! Y! Z!
    'There is no more trouble ahead,
'Sorrow or any such thing –
      'For Mr and Mrs Discobbolos!'

MR AND MRS DISCOBBOLOS

SECOND PART

I

Mr and Mrs Discobbolos
   Lived on the top of the wall,
  For twenty years, a month and a day,
  Till their hair had grown all pearly gray,
   And their teeth began to fall.
They never were ill, or at all dejected,
By all admired, and by some respected,
   Till Mrs Discobbolos said,
    'O, W! X! Y! Z!
    'It has just come into my head,
  'We have no more room at all –
     'Darling Mr Discobbolos!

II

'Look at our six fine boys!
  'And our six sweet girls so fair!
'Upon this wall they have all been born,
'And not one of the twelve has happened to fall
  'Through my maternal care!
'Surely they should not pass their lives
'Without any chance of husbands or wives!'
   And Mrs Discobbolos said,
    'O, W! X! Y! Z!
  'Did it never come into your head
'That our lives must be lived elsewhere,
    Dearest Mr Discobbolos?

III

'They have never been at a ball,
  'Nor have even seen a bazaar!
'Nor have heard folks say in a tone all hearty
"What loves of girls (at a garden party)
  Those Misses Discobbolos are!"
'Morning and night it drives me wild
'To think of the fate of each darling child!'
    But Mr Discobbolos said,
      'O, W! X! Y! Z!
      'What has come to your fiddledum head!
'What a runcible goose you are!
            'Octopod Mrs Discobbolos!'

Suddenly Mr Discobbolos
    Slid from the top of the wall;
  And beneath it he dug a dreadful trench,
  And filled it with dynamite, gunpowder gench,
    And aloud he began to call –
'Let the wild bee sing,
'And the blue bird hum!
'For the end of your lives has certainly come!'
    And Mrs Discobbolos said,
      'O, W! X! Y! Z!
      'We shall presently all be dead,
  'On this ancient runcible wall,
            'Terrible Mr Discobbolos!'

Pensively, Mr Discobbolos
   Sat with his back to the wall;
  He lighted a match, and fired the train,
  And the mortified mountain echoed again
   To the sound of an awful fall!
And all the Discobbolos family flew
In thousands of bits to the sky so blue,
   And no one was left to have said,
   'O, W! X! Y! Z!
  'Has it come into anyone's head
  'That the end has happened to all
      'Of the whole of the Clan Discobbolos?'

IV
MRS JAYPHER'S WISDOM

MRS JAYPHER

A poem to be read 'sententiously and with grave importance':

Mrs Jaypher found a wafer
Which she stuck upon a note;
This she took and gave the cook.
Then she went and bought a boat
Which she paddled down the stream
Shouting: 'Ice produces cream,
Beer when churned produces butter!
Henceforth all the words I utter
Distant ages thus shall note –
From the Jaypher Wisdom-Boat.'

DINGLE BANK

He lived at Dingle Bank – he did; –
   He lived at Dingle Bank;
And in his garden was one Quail,
   Four tulips and a Tank:
And from his windows he could see
The otion and the River Dee.

His house stood on a Cliff, – it did,
   Its aspic it was cool;
And many thousand little boys
   Resorted to his school
Where if of progress they could boast
He gave them heaps of buttered toast.

But he grew rabid-wroth, he did,
   If they neglected books,
And dragged them to adjacent cliffs
   With beastly Button Hooks,
And there with fatuous glee he threw
Them down into the otion blue.

And in the sea they swam, they did, –
   All playfully about,
And some eventually became
   Sponges or special trout: –
But Liverpool doth all bewail
Their fate; – likewise his Garden Quail.

THE NEW VESTMENTS

There lived an old man in the Kingdom of Tess,
Who invented a purely original dress;
And when it was perfectly made and complete,
He opened the door, and walked into the street.

By way of a hat, he'd a loaf of Brown Bread,
In the middle of which he inserted his head; –
His Shirt was made up of no end of dead Mice,
The warmth of whose skins was quite fluffy and nice; –
His Drawers were of Rabbit-skins; – so were his Shoes; –
His Stockings were skins, – but it is not known whose; –
His Waistcoat and Trowsers were made of Pork Chops; –
His Buttons were Jujubes, and Chocolate Drops; –
His Coat was all Pancakes with Jam for a border,
And a girdle of Biscuits to keep it in order;
And he wore over all, as a screen from bad weather,
A Cloak of green Cabbage-leaves stitched all together.

He had walked a short way, when he heard a great noise,
Of all sorts of Beasticles, Birdlings, and Boys; –
And from every long street and dark lane in the town
Beasts, Birdles, and Boys in a tumult rushed down.
Two Cows and a half ate his Cabbage-leaf Cloak; –
Four Apes seized his Girdle, which vanished like smoke; –
Three Kids ate up half of his Pancaky Coat, –
And the tails were devour'd by an ancient He Goat; –
An army of Dogs in a twinkling tore *up* his
Pork Waistcoat and Trowsers to give to their Puppies; –
And while they were growling, and mumbling the Chops,
Ten Boys prigged the Jujubes and Chocolate Drops. –
He tried to run back to his house, but in vain,
For Scores of fat Pigs came again and again; –
They rushed out of stables and hovels and doors, –
They tore off his stockings, his shoes, and his drawers; –

And now from the housetops with screechings descend,
Striped, spotted, white, black, and gray Cats without end,
They jumped on his shoulders and knocked off his hat, –
When Crows, Ducks, and Hens made a mincemeat of that; –
They speedily flew at his sleeves in a trice,
And utterly tore up his Shirt of dead Mice; –
They swallowed the last of his Shirt with a squall, –
Whereon he ran home with no clothes on at all.

And he said to himself as he bolted the door,
'I will not wear a similar dress any more,
'Any more, any more, any more, never more!'

THE TWO OLD BACHELORS

Two old Bachelors were living in one house;
One caught a Muffin, the other caught a Mouse.
Said he who caught the Muffin to him who caught the Mouse, –
'This happens just in time! For we've nothing in the house,
'Save a tiny slice of lemon and a teaspoonful of honey,
'And what to do for dinner – since we haven't any money?
'And what can we expect if we haven't any dinner,
'But to lose our teeth and eyelashes and keep on growing
    thinner?'

Said he who caught the Mouse to him who caught the Muffin, –
'We might cook this little Mouse, if we only had some Stuffin'!
'If we had but Sage and Onion we could do extremely well,
'But how to get that Stuffin' it is difficult to tell!' –

Those two old Bachelors ran quickly to the town
And asked for Sage and Onions as they wandered up and down;
They borrowed two large Onions, but no Sage was to be found
In the Shops, or in the Market, or in all the Gardens round.

But some one said, – 'A hill there is, a little to the north,
'And to its purpledicular top a narrow way leads forth; –
'And there among the rugged rocks abides an ancient Sage, –

'An earnest Man, who reads all day a most perplexing page.
'Climb up, and seize him by the toes! – all studious as he sits, –
'And pull him down, – and chop him into endless little bits!
'Then mix him with your Onion, (cut up likewise into Scraps,) –
'When your Stuffin' will be ready – and very good: perhaps.'

Those two old Bachelors without loss of time
The nearly purpledicular crags at once began to climb;
And at the top, among the rocks, all seated in a nook,
They saw that Sage, a reading of a most enormous book.
'You earnest Sage!' aloud they cried, 'your book you've read
    enough in! –
'We wish to chop you into bits to mix you into Stuffin'!' –

But that old Sage looked calmly up, and with his awful book,
At those two Bachelors' bald heads a certain aim he took; –
And over crag and precipice they rolled promiscuous down, –
At once they rolled, and never stopped in lane or field or town, –
And when they reached their house, they found (besides their
    want of Stuffin',)
The Mouse had fled; – and, previously, had eaten up the Muffin.

They left their home in silence by the once convivial door.
And from that hour those Bachelors were never heard of more.

THE POBBLE WHO HAS NO TOES

I

The Pobble who has no toes
  Had once as many as we;
When they said, 'Some day you may lose them all;' –
  He replied, – 'Fish fiddle de-dee!'
And his Aunt Jobiska made him drink,
Lavender water tinged with pink,
For she said, 'The World in general knows
There's nothing so good for a Pobble's toes!'

II

The Pobble who has no toes,
  Swam across the Bristol Channel;
But before he set out he wrapped his nose,
  In a piece of scarlet flannel.
For his Aunt Jobiska said, 'No harm
Can come to his toes if his nose is warm;
And it's perfectly known that a Pobble's toes
Are safe, – provided he minds his nose.'

III

The Pobble swam fast and well
  And when boats or ships came near him
He tinkledy-binkledy-winkled a bell
  So that all the world could hear him.

And all the Sailors and Admirals cried,
When they saw him nearing the further side, –
'He has gone to fish, for his Aunt Jobiska's
Runcible Cat with crimson whiskers!'

IV

But before he touched the shore,
    The shore of the Bristol Channel,
A sea-green Porpoise carried away
    His wrapper of scarlet flannel.
And when he came to observe his feet
Formerly garnished with toes so neat
His face at once became forlorn
On perceiving that all his toes were gone!

V

And nobody ever knew
    From that dark day to the present,
Whoso had taken the Pobble's toes,
    In a manner so far from pleasant.
Whether the shrimps or crawfish gray,
Or crafty Mermaids stole them away –
Nobody knew; and nobody knows
How the Pobble was robbed of his twice five toes!

VI

The Pobble who has no toes
    Was placed in a friendly Bark,
And they rowed him back, and carried him up,
    To his Aunt Jobiska's Park.
And she made him a feast at his earnest wish
Of eggs and buttercups fried with fish; –
And she said, – 'It's a fact the whole world knows,
That Pobbles are happier without their toes.'

AN EPITAPH

Beneath these high Cathedral stairs
Lie the remains of Susan Pares,
Her name was Wiggs it was not Pares
But Pares was put to rhyme with stairs.

THE LAST OF MRS JAYPHER

Mrs Jaypher said it's safer
If you've lemons in your head
First to eat a pound of meat
And then to go at once to bed.

V

ABSTEMIOUS ASSES, ZEALOUS ZEBRAS
and Others

'And now I go with a large book and a
piece of chalk to school every day like a
good little boy.'

The Absolutely Abstemious Ass,
who resided in a Barrel, and only lived on
Soda Water and Pickled Cucumbers.

The Bountiful Beetle,
who always carried a Green Umbrella when it didn't rain,
and left it at home when it did.

The Comfortable Confidential Cow,
who sate in her Red Morocco Arm Chair and
toasted her own Bread at the parlour Fire.

The Dolomphious Duck,
who caught Spotted Frogs for her dinner
with a Runcible Spoon.

The Enthusiastic Elephant,
who ferried himself across the water with the
Kitchen Poker and a New pair of Ear-rings.

The Fizzgiggious Fish,
who always walked about upon Stilts.
because he had no legs.

The Goodnatured Grey Gull,
who carried the Old Owl, and his Crimson Carpet-bag,
across the river, because he could not swim.

The Hasty Higgeldipiggledy Hen,
who went to market in a Blue Bonnet and Shawl,
and bought a Fish for her Supper...

The Inventive Indian,
who caught a Remarkable Rabbit in a
Stupendous Silver Spoon.

The Judicious Jubilant Jay,
who did up her Back Hair every morning with a Wreath of Roses
Three feathers, and a Gold Pin.

The Kicking Kangaroo,
who wore a Pale Pink Muslin dress
with Blue spots.

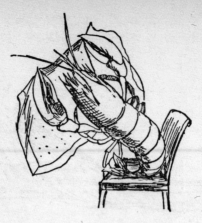

The Lively Learned Lobster,
who mended his own Clothes with
a Needle and Thread.

The Melodious Meritorious Mouse,
who played a merry minuet on the
Piano·forte.

The Nutritious Newt,
who purchased a Round Plum-pudding
for his grand-daughter.

The Obsequious Ornamental Ostrich,
who wore Boots to keep his
feet quite dry.

The Perpendicular Purple Polly,
who read the Newspaper and ate Parsnip Pie
with his Spectacles.

The Queer Querulous Quail,
who smoked a Pipe of tobacco on the top of
a Tin Tea-kettle.

The Rural Runcible Raven,
who wore a White Wig and flew away
with the Carpet Broom.

The Scroobious Snake,
who always wore a Hat on his Head, for
fear he should bite anybody.

The Tumultuous Tom-tommy Tortoise,
who beat a Drum all day long in the
middle of the wilderness.

The Umbrageous Umbrella-maker,
whose Face nobody ever saw, because it was
always covered by his Umbrella.

The Visibly Vicious Vulture,
who wrote some Verses to a Veal-cutlet in a
Volume bound in Vellum.

The Worrying Whizzing Wasp,
who stood on a Table, and played sweetly on a
Flute with a Morning Cap.

The Excellent Double-extra XX
imbibing King Xerxes, who lived a
long while ago.

The Yonghy-Bonghy-Bò,
whose Head was ever so much bigger than his
Body, and whose Hat was rather small.

The Zigzag Zealous Zebra,
who carried five Monkeys on his back all
the way to Jellibolee.

AN EXTRACT FROM THE *NONSENSE GAZETTE* FOR AUGUST 1870

Our readers will be interested in the following communications from our valued and learned contributor, Professor Bosh, whose labours in the fields of Culinary and Botanical science, are so well known to all the world. The first three Articles richly merit to be added to the Domestic cookery of every family; those which follow, claim the attention of all Botanists, and we are happy to be able through Dr Bosh's kindness to present our readers with illustrations of his discoveries. All the new flowers are found in the valley of Verrikwier, near the lake of Oddgrow, and on the summit of the hill Orfeltugg.

Three Receipts for Domestic Cookery

TO MAKE AN AMBLONGUS PIE

Take 4 pounds (say 4½ pounds) of fresh Amblongusses, and put them in a small pipkin.

Cover them with water and boil them for 8 hours incessantly, after which add 2 pints of new milk, and proceed to boil for 4 hours more.

When you have ascertained that the Amblongusses are quite soft, take them out and place them in a wide pan, taking care to shake them well previously.

Grate some nutmeg over the surface, and cover them carefully with powdered gingerbread, curry-powder, and a sufficient quantity of Cayenne pepper.

Remove the pan into the next room, and place it on the floor. Bring it back again, and let it simmer for three-quarters of an hour. Shake the pan violently till all the Amblongusses have become of a pale purple colour.

Then, having prepared the paste, insert the whole carefully, adding at the same time a small pigeon, 2 slices of beef, 4 cauliflowers, and any number of oysters.

129

Watch patiently till the crust begins to rise, and add a pinch of salt from time to time.

Serve up in a clean dish, and throw the whole out of the window as fast as possible.

TO MAKE CRUMBOBBLIOUS CUTLETS

Procure some strips of beef, and having cut them into the smallest possible slices, proceed to cut them still smaller, eight or perhaps nine times.

When the whole is thus minced, brush it up hastily with a new clothes-brush, and stir round rapidly and capriciously with a salt-spoon or a soup-ladle.

Place the whole in a saucepan, and remove it to a sunny place, – say the roof of the house if free from sparrows or other birds, – and leave it there for about a week.

At the end of that time add a little lavender, some oil of almonds, and a few herring-bones; and then cover the whole with 4 gallons of clarified crumbobblious sauce, when it will be ready for use.

Cut it into the shape of ordinary cutlets, and serve up in a clean tablecloth or dinner-napkin.

TO MAKE GOSKY PATTIES

Take a Pig, three or four years of age, and tie him by the off-hind leg to a post. Place 5 pounds of currants, 3 of sugar, 2 pecks of peas, 18 roast chestnuts, a candle, and six bushels of turnips, within his reach; if he eats these, constantly provide him with more.

Then procure some cream, some slices of Cheshire cheese, four quires of foolscap paper, and a packet of black pins. Work the whole into a paste, and spread it out to dry on a sheet of clean brown waterproof linen.

When the paste is perfectly dry, but not before, proceed to beat the Pig violently, with the handle of a large broom. If he squeals, beat him again.

Visit the paste and beat the Pig alternately for some days, and ascertain if at the end of that period the whole is about to turn into Gosky Patties.

If it does not then, it never will; and in that case the Pig may be let loose, and the whole process may be considered as finished.

Bottlephorkia Spoonifolia

Smalltoothcombia Domestica

Bluebottlia Buzztilentia

Pollybirdia Singularis

Phattfacia Stupenda

Plumbunnia Nutritiosa

Manypeeplia Upsidownia

Guittara Pensilis

Cockatooca Superba

Baccopipia Gracilis

Fishia Marina

Piggiawiggia Pyramidalis

VI
TWO STORIES

THE STORY OF THE FOUR LITTLE CHILDREN WHO WENT ROUND THE WORLD

Once upon a time, a long while ago, there were four little people whose names were

VIOLET,   SLINGSBY,   GUY,   and LIONEL;

and they all thought they should like to see the world. So they bought a large boat to sail quite round the world by sea, and then they were to come back on the other side by land. The boat was painted blue with green spots, and the sail was yellow with red stripes; and when they set off, they only took a small Cat to steer and look after the boat, besides an elderly Quangle-Wangle, who had to cook the dinner and make the tea; for which purposes they took a large kettle.

137

For the first ten days they sailed on beautifully, and found plenty to eat, as there were lots of fish, and they had only to take them out of the sea with a long spoon, when the Quangle-Wangle instantly cooked them, and the Pussy-cat was fed with the bones, with which she expressed herself pleased on the whole, so that all the party were very happy.

During the day-time, Violet chiefly occupied herself in putting salt-water into a churn, while her three brothers churned it violently, in the hope that it would turn into butter, which it seldom, if ever did; and in the evening they all retired into the Tea-kettle, where they all managed to sleep very comfortably, while Pussy and the Quangle-Wangle managed the boat.

After a time they saw some land at a distance; and when they came to it, they found it was an island made of water quite surrounded by earth. Besides that, it was bordered by evanescent isthmusses with a great Gulf-stream running about all over it, so that it was perfectly beautiful, and contained only a single tree, 503 feet high.

When they had landed, they walked about, but found to their great surprise that the island was quite full of veal-cutlets and chocolate-drops, and nothing else. So they all climbed up the single high tree to discover, if possible, if there were any people; but having remained on the top of the tree for a week, and not seeing anybody, they naturally concluded that there were no inhabitants, and accordingly when they came down they loaded the boat with two thousand veal-cutlets and a million of chocolate drops, and these afforded them sustenance for more than a month, during which time they pursued their voyage with the utmost delight and apathy.

After this they came to a shore where there were no less than sixty-five great red parrots with blue tails, sitting on a rail all of a row, and all fast asleep. And I am sorry to say that the Pussy-cat and the Quangle-Wangle crept softly and bit off the tail-feathers of all the sixty-five parrots, for which Violet reproved them both severely.

Notwithstanding which, she proceeded to insert all the feathers, two hundred and sixty in number, in her bonnet, thereby causing it to have a lovely and glittering appearance, highly prepossessing and efficacious.

The next thing that happened to them was in a narrow part of the sea, which was so entirely full of fishes that the boat could go on no further; so they remained there about six weeks, till they had eaten nearly all the fishes, which were Soles, and all ready-cooked and covered with shrimp sauce, so that there was no trouble whatever. And as the few fishes who remained uneaten complained of the cold, as well as of the difficulty they had in getting any sleep on account of the extreme noise made by the Arctic Bears and the Tropical Turnspits which frequented the neighbourhood in great numbers, Violet most amiably knitted a small woollen frock for several of the fishes, and Slingsby administered some opium drops to them, through which kindness they became quite warm and slept soundly.

Then they came to a country which was wholly covered with immense Orange-trees of a vast size, and quite full of fruit. So they all landed, taking with them the Tea-kettle, intending to gather some of the Oranges and place them in it. But while they were busy about this, a most dreadfully high wind rose, and blew out most of the Parrot-tail feathers from Violet's bonnet. That, however, was nothing compared with the calamity of the Oranges falling down on their heads by millions and millions, which thumped and bumped and bumped and thumped them all so seriously that they were obliged to run as hard as they

could for their lives, besides that the sound of the Oranges rattling on the Tea-kettle was of the most fearful and amazing nature.

Nevertheless they got safely to the boat, although considerably vexed and hurt; and the Quangle-Wangle's right foot was so knocked about that he had to sit with his head in his slipper for at least a week.

This event made them all for a time rather melancholy, and perhaps they might never have become less so, had not Lionel, with a most praiseworthy devotion and perseverance, continued to stand on one leg and whistle to them in a loud and lively manner, which diverted the whole party so extremely, that they gradually recovered their spirits, and agreed that whenever they should reach home they would subscribe towards a testimonial to Lionel, entirely made of Gingerbread and Raspberries, as an earnest token of their sincere and grateful infection.

After sailing on calmly for several more days, they came to another country, where they were much pleased and surprised to see a countless multitude of white Mice with red eyes, all sitting in a great circle, slowly eating Custard Pudding with the most satisfactory and polite demeanour.

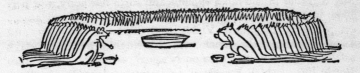

And as the four Travellers were rather hungry, being tired of eating nothing but Soles and Oranges for so long a period, they held a council as to the propriety of asking the Mice for some of their Pudding in a humble and affecting manner, by which they could hardly be otherwise than gratified. It was agreed therefore that Guy should go and ask the Mice, which he immediately did; and the result was that they gave a Walnut-shell only half full of Custard diluted with water. Now, this displeased Guy, who said, 'Out of such a lot of Pudding as you have got, I must say you might have spared a somewhat larger quantity!' But no sooner had he finished speaking than all the Mice turned round at once, and sneezed at him in an appalling and vindictive manner, (and it is impossible to imagine a more scroobious and unpleasant sound than that caused by the simultaneous sneezing of many millions of angry Mice,) so that Guy rushed back to the boat, having first shied his cap into the middle of the Custard Pudding, by which means he completely spoiled the Mice's dinner.

By-and-by the Four Children came to a country where there were no houses, but only an incredibly innumerable number of large bottles without corks, and of a dazzling and sweetly susceptible blue colour. Each of these blue bottles contained a Blue-Bottle-Fly, and all these interesting animals live continually together in the most copious and rural harmony, nor perhaps in many parts of the world is such perfect and abject happiness to be found. Violet, and Slingsby, and Guy, and Lionel, were greatly struck with this singular and instructive settlement, and having previously asked permission of the Blue-Bottle-Flies (which was most courteously granted), the Boat was drawn up to the shore and they proceeded to make tea in front of the Bottles; but as they had no tea-leaves, they merely

placed some pebbles in the hot water, and the Quangle-Wangle played some tunes over it on an Accordion, by which of course tea was made directly, and of the very best quality.

The Four Children then entered into conversation with the Blue-Bottle-Flies, who discoursed in a placid and genteel manner, though with a slightly buzzing accent, chiefly owing to the fact that they each held a small clothes-brush between their teeth, which naturally occasioned a fizzy extraneous utterance.

'Why,' said Violet, 'would you kindly inform us, do you reside in bottles? and if in bottles at all, why not rather in green or purple, or indeed in yellow bottles?'

To which questions a very aged Blue-Bottle-Fly answered, 'We found the bottles here all ready to live in, that is to say, our great-great-great-great-great-grandfathers did, so we occupied them at once. And when the winter comes on, we turn the bottles upsidedown, and consequently rarely feel the cold at all, and you know very well that this could not be the case with bottles of any other colour than blue.'

'Of course it could not', said Slingsby; 'but if we may take the liberty of inquiring, on what do you chiefly subsist?'

'Mainly on Oyster-patties,' said the Blue-Bottle-Fly, 'and, when these are scarce, on Raspberry Vinegar and Russian leather boiled down to a jelly.'

'How delicious!' said Guy.

To which Lionel added, 'Huzz!' and all the Blue-Bottle-Flies said 'Buzz!'

At this time, an elderly Fly said it was the hour for the Evening-song to be sung; and on a signal being given all the Blue-Bottle-Flies began to buzz at once in a sumptuous and sonorous manner, the melodious and mucilaginous sounds echoing all over the waters, and resounding across the tumultuous tops of the transitory Titmice upon the intervening and verdant mountains, with a serene and sickly suavity only known to the truly virtuous. The Moon was shining slobaciously from the star-bespringled sky, while her light irrigated the smooth and shiny sides and wings and backs of the Blue-Bottle-Flies with a peculiar and trivial splendour, while all nature cheerfully responded to the cerulæan and conspicuous circumstances.

In many long-after years, the four little Travellers looked back to that evening as one of the happiest in all their lives, and it was already past midnight, when – the Sail of the Boat having been set up by the Quangle-Wangle, the Tea-kettle and Churn placed in their respective positions, and the Pussy-cat stationed at the Helm – the Children each took a last and affectionate farewell of the Blue-Bottle-Flies, who walked down in a body to the water's edge to see the Travellers embark.

As a token of parting respect and esteem, Violet made a curtsey quite down to the ground, and stuck one of her few remaining Parrot-tail feathers into the back hair of the most pleasing of the Blue-Bottle-Flies, while Slingsby, Guy and

Lionel offered them three small boxes, containing respectively, Black Pins, Dried Figs and Epsom Salts: and thus they left that happy shore for ever.

Overcome by their feelings, the Four little Travellers instantly jumped into the Tea-kettle, and fell fast asleep. But all along the shore for many hours there was distinctly heard a sound of severely suppressed sobs, and of a vague multitude of living creatures using their pocket-handkerchiefs in a subdued simultaneous snuffle – lingering sadly along the wallopping waves as the boat sailed farther and farther away from the Land of the Happy Blue-Bottle-Flies.

Nothing particular occurred for some days after these events, except that as the Travellers were passing a low tract of sand, they perceived an unusual and gratifying spectacle, namely, a large number of Crabs and Crawfish – perhaps six or seven

146

hundred – sitting by the water-side, and endeavouring to disentangle a vast heap of pale pink worsted, which they moistened at intervals with a fluid composed of Lavender-water and White-wine Negus.

'Can we be of any service to you, O crusty Crabbies?' said the Four Children.

'Thank you kindly,' said the Crabs, consecutively. 'We are trying to make some worsted Mittens, but do not know how.'

On which Violet, who was perfectly acquainted with the art of mitten-making, said to the Crabs, 'Do your claws unscrew, or are they fixtures?'

'They are all made to unscrew,' said the Crabs, and forthwith they deposited a great pile of claws close to the boat, with which Violet uncombed all the pale pink worsted, and then made the loveliest Mittens with it you can imagine. These the Crabs, having resumed and screwed on their claws, placed cheerfully upon their wrists, and walked away rapidly on their hind-legs, warbling songs with a silvery voice and in a minor key.

After this the four little people sailed on again till they came to a vast and wide plain of astonishing dimensions, on which nothing whatever could be discovered at first; but as the Travellers walked onward, there appeared in the extreme and dim distance a single object, which on a nearer approach, and on an accurately cutaneous inspection, seemed to be somebody in a large white wig sitting on an arm-chair made of Sponge Cakes and Oyster-shells. 'It does not quite look like a human being,' said Violet, doubtfully; nor could they make out what it really was, till the Quangle-Wangle (who had previously been round the world), exclaimed softly in a loud voice, 'It is the Co-operative Cauliflower!'

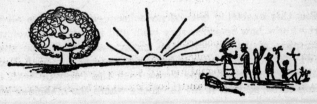

And so in truth it was, and they soon found that what they had taken for an immense wig was in reality the top of the cauliflower, and that he had no feet at all, being able to walk tolerably well with a fluctuating and graceful movement on a single cabbage stalk, an accomplishment which naturally saved him the expense of stockings and shoes.

Presently, while the whole party from the boat was gazing at him with mingled affection and disgust, he suddenly arose, and in a somewhat plumdomphious manner hurried off towards the setting sun, – his steps supported by two superincumbent confidential cucumbers, and a large number of Waterwagtails proceeding in advance of him by three-and-three in a row – till he finally disappeared on the brink of the western sky in a crystal cloud of sudorific sand.

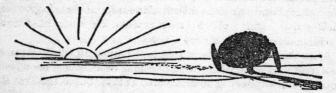

So remarkable a sight of course impressed the Four Children very deeply; and they returned immediately to their boat with a strong sense of undeveloped asthma and a great appetite.

Shortly after this the Travellers were obliged to sail directly below some high overhanging rocks, from the top of one of which, a particularly odious little boy, dressed in rose-coloured knickerbockers, and with a pewter plate upon his head, threw an enormous Pumpkin at the boat, by which it was instantly upset.

But this upsetting was of no consequence, because all the party knew how to swim very well, and in fact they preferred swimming about till after the moon rose, when, the water growing chilly, they sponge-taneously entered the boat. Meanwhile the Quangle-Wangle threw back the Pumpkin with immense force, so that it hit the rocks where the malicious little

boy in rose-coloured knickerbockers was sitting, when, being quite full of Lucifer-matches, the Pumpkin exploded surreptitiously into a thousand bits, whereon the rocks instantly took fire, and the odious little boy became unpleasantly hotter and hotter and hotter, till his knickerbockers were turned quite green, and his nose was burned off.

Two or three days after this had happened, they came to another place, where they found nothing at all except some wide and deep pits full of Mulberry Jam. This is the property of the tiny Yellow-nosed Apes who abound in these districts, and who store up the Mulberry Jam for their food in winter, when they mix it with pellucid pale periwinkle soup, and serve it out in Wedgwood China bowls, which grow freely all over that part of the country. Only one of the Yellow-nosed Apes was on the spot, and he was fast asleep: yet the Four Travellers and the Quangle-Wangle and Pussy were so terrified by the violence and sanguinary sound of his snoring, that they merely took a small cupful of the Jam, and returned to re-embark in their Boat without delay.

What was their horror on seeing the boat (including the Churn and the Tea-kettle), in the mouth of an enormous Seeze Pyder, an aquatic and ferocious creature truly dreadful to behold, and happily only met with in those excessive longitudes. In a moment the beautiful boat was bitten into fifty-five-thousand-million-hundred-billion bits, and it instantly became quite clear

149

that Violet, Slingsby, Guy and Lionel could no longer preliminate their voyage by sea.

The Four Travellers were therefore obliged to resolve on pursuing their wanderings by land, and very fortunately there happened to pass by at that moment, an elderly Rhinoceros, on which they seized; and all four mounting on his back, the Quangle-Wangle sitting on his horn and holding on by his ears, and the Pussy-cat swinging at the end of his tail, they set off, having only four small beans and three pounds of mashed potatoes to last through their whole journey.

They were, however, able to catch numbers of the chickens and turkeys, and other birds who incessantly alighted on the head of the Rhinoceros for the purpose of gathering the seeds of the rhododendron plants which grew there, and these creatures they cooked in the most translucent and satisfactory manner, by means of a fire lighted on the end of the Rhinoceros' back. A crowd of Kangaroos and Gigantic Cranes accompanied them, from feelings of curiosity and complacency, so that they were never at a loss for company, and went onward as it were in a sort of profuse and triumphant procession.

Thus, in less than eighteen weeks, they all arrived safely at home, where they were received by their admiring relatives with joy tempered with contempt; and where they finally resolved to carry out the rest of their travelling plans at some more favourable opportunity.

As for the Rhinoceros, in token of their grateful adherence, they had him killed and stuffed directly, and then set him up outside the door of their father's house as a Diaphanous Doorscraper.

A MORAL FABLE

Once upon a time three poor students, all very near-sighted, and each possessing a single pair of horn-rimmed spectacles, set out to walk to a remote university, for the purpose of competing for a professorship.

On the way, while sleeping by the road-side, a thief stole their three pairs of horn-rimmed spectacles.

Waking, their distress was great: they stumbled, they fell, they lost their way; and night was at hand, when they met a pedlar.

'Have you any spectacles?' said the three miserable students.

'Yes,' said the pedlar, 'exactly three pairs; but they are set in gold, and with magnificent workmanship; in fact, they were made for the king, and they cost so much —'

'Such a sum,' said the students, 'is absurd; it is nearly as much as we possess.'

'I cannot,' the pedlar replied, 'take less; but here is an ivory-handled frying-pan which I can let you have for a trifling sum, and I strongly recommend you to buy it because it is such an astonishing bargain, and you may never again chance to meet with a similarly joyful opportunity.'

Said the eldest of the three students, 'I will grope my way on as I can. It is ridiculous to buy a pair of this man's spectacles at such a price.'

'And I,' said the second, 'am determined to purchase the ivory-handled frying-pan; it costs little, and will be very useful, and I may never again have such an extraordinary bargain.'

But the youngest of the three, undisturbed by the laughter

of the two others, bought the gold-rimmed sumptuous spectacles, and was soon out of sight.

Thereon, No. 1 set off slowly, but, falling into a ditch by reason of his blindness, broke his leg, and was carried back, by a charitable passer-by in a cart, to his native town.

No. 2 wandered on, but lost his way inextricably, and, after much suffering, was obliged to sell his ivory-handled frying-pan at a great loss, to enable him to return home.

No. 3 reached the University, gained the prize, and was made Professor of Grumphiology, with a house and fixed salary, and lived happily ever after.

Moral. – To pay much for what is most useful, is wiser than to pay little for what is not so.

VII
AN EPISODE OF NOSES

'... this is amazingly like; add only – that both my knees are fractured from being run over which has made them peculiarly crooked – that my neck is singularly long – a most elephantine nose – & a disposition to tumble here & there – owing to being half blind and you may very well imagine my tout ensemble.

*From an unpublished letter from Edward Lear
to C. Empson (1831).*

There was an old man of West Dumpet,
Who possessed a large nose like a trumpet;
When he blew it aloud, it astonished the crowd,
And was heard through the whole of West Dumpet.

There is a young lady, whose nose,
Continually prospers and grows;
When it grew out of sight, she exclaimed in a fright,
'Oh! Farewell to the end of my nose!'

There was an old man in a barge,
Whose nose was exceedingly large;
But in fishing by night, it supported a light,
Which helped that old man in a barge.

There was a Young Lady whose nose,
Was so long that it reached to her toes;
So she hired an Old Lady, whose conduct was steady,
To carry that wonderful nose.

There was an Old Person of Tring,
Who embellished his nose with a ring;
He gazed at the moon, every evening in June,
That ecstatic Old Person of Tring.

There was an Old Man with a nose,
Who said, 'If you choose to suppose,
That my nose is too long, you are certainly wrong!'
That remarkable Man with a nose.

There was an old person of Cassel,
Whose nose finished off in a tassel;
But they call'd out, 'Oh well! – don't it look like a bell!'
Which perplexed that old person of Cassel.

There was an Old Man, on whose nose,
Most birds of the air could repose;
But they all flew away, at the closing of day,
Which relieved that Old Man and his nose.

VIII
TWO TALES OF
THE JUMBLIES

THE JUMBLIES

I

They went to sea in a Sieve, they did,
   In a Sieve they went to sea:
In spite of all their friends could say,
On a winter's morn, on a stormy day,
   In a Sieve they went to sea!
And when the Sieve turned round and round,
And every one cried, 'You'll all be drowned!'
They called aloud, 'Our Sieve ain't big,
But we don't care a button! we don't care a fig!
   In a Sieve we'll go to sea!'
     Far and few, far and few,
      Are the lands where the Jumblies live;
      Their heads are green, and their hands are blue,
      And they went to sea in a Sieve.

II

They sailed away in a Sieve, they did,
   In a Sieve they sailed so fast,
With only a beautiful pea-green veil
Tied with a riband by way of a sail,
   To a small tobacco-pipe mast;

And every one said, who saw them go,
'O won't they be soon upset, you know!
For the sky is dark, and the voyage is long,
And happen what may, it's extremely wrong
   In a Sieve to sail so fast!'
     Far and few, far and few,
       Are the lands where the Jumblies live;
       Their heads are green, and their hands are blue,
       And they went to sea in a Sieve.

III

The water it soon came in, it did,
   The water it soon came in; '
So to keep them dry, they wrapped their feet
In a pinky paper all folded neat,
   And they fastened it down with a pin.
And they passed the night in a crockery-jar,
And each of them said, 'How wise we are!
Though the sky be dark, and the voyage be long,
Yet we never can think we were rash or wrong,
   While round in our Sieve we spin!'
     Far and few, far and few,
       Are the lands where the Jumblies live;
       Their heads are green, and their hands are blue,
       And they went to sea in a Sieve.

IV

And all night long they sailed away;
   And when the sun went down,
They whistled and warbled a moony song
To the echoing sound of a coppery gong,
   In the shade of the mountains brown.
'O Timballo! How happy we are,
When we live in a sieve and a crockery-jar,
And all night long in the moonlight pale,
We sail away with a pea-green sail,

In the shade of the mountains brown!'
   Far and few, far and few,
     Are the lands where the Jumblies live;
    Their heads are green, and their hands are blue,
     And they went to sea in a Sieve.

V

They sailed to the Western Sea, they did,
  To a land all covered with trees,
And they bought an Owl, and a useful Cart,
And a pound of Rice, and a Cranberry Tart,
  And a hive of silvery Bees.
And they bought a Pig, and some green Jack-daws,
And a lovely Monkey with lollipop paws,
And forty bottles of Ring-Bo-Ree,
  And no end of Stilton Cheese.
   Far and few, far and few,
     Are the lands where the Jumblies live;
    Their heads are green, and their hands are blue,
     And they went to sea in a Sieve.

VI

And in twenty years they all came back,
  In twenty years or more,
And every one said, 'How tall they've grown!
For they've been to the Lakes, and the Torrible Zone,
  And the hills of the Chankly Bore;'
And they drank their health, and gave them a feast
Of dumplings made of beautiful yeast;
And every one said, 'If we only live,
We too will go to sea in a Sieve, –
  To the hills of the Chankly Bore!'
   Far and few, far and few,
     Are the lands where the Jumblies live;
    Their heads are green, and their hands are blue,
     And they went to sea in a Sieve.

THE DONG WITH A LUMINOUS NOSE

When awful darkness and silence reign
Over the great Gromboolian plain,
  Through the long, long wintry nights; –
When the angry breakers roar
As they beat on the rocky shore; –
  When Storm-clouds brood on the towering heights
Of the Hills of the Chankly Bore; –

Then, through the vast and gloomy dark,
There moves what seems a fiery spark,
  A lonely spark with silvery rays
  Piercing the coal-black night, –
  A Meteor strange and bright: –
Hither and thither the vision strays,
  A single lurid light.

Slowly it wanders, – pauses, – creeps, –
Anon it sparkles, – flashes and leaps;
And ever as onward it gleaming goes
A light on the Bong-tree stems it throws.
And those who watch at that midnight hour
From Hall or Terrace, or lofty Tower,

Cry, as the wild light passes along, –
   'The Dong! – the Dong!
  'The wandering Dong through the forest goes!
   'The Dong! the Dong!
  'The Dong with a luminous Nose!'

   Long years ago
  The Dong was happy and gay,
Till he fell in love with a Jumbly Girl
  Who came to those shores one day,
For the Jumblies came in a sieve, they did, –
Landing at eve near the Zemmery Fidd
   Where the Oblong Oysters grow,
  And the rocks are smooth and gray.
And all the woods and the valleys rang
With the Chorus they daily and nightly sang, –
    'Far and few, far and few,
    Are the lands where the Jumblies live;
    Their heads are green, and their hands are blue
    And they went to sea in a sieve.'

Happily, happily passed those days!
   While the cheerful Jumblies staid;
  They danced in circlets all night long,
  To the plaintive pipe of the lively Dong,
   In moonlight, shine, or shade.
For day and night he was always there
By the side of the Jumbly Girl so fair,
With her sky-blue hands, and her sea-green hair.
Till the morning came of that hateful day
When the Jumblies sailed in their sieve away,
And the Dong was left on the cruel shore
Gazing – gazing for evermore, –
Ever keeping his weary eyes on
That pea-green sail on the far horizon, –
Singing the Jumbly Chorus still
As he sate all day on the grassy hill, –

> '*Far and few, far and few,*
> *Are the lands where the Jumblies live;*
> *Their heads are green, and their hands are blue,*
> *And they went to sea in a sieve.*'

But when the sun was low in the West,
  The Dong arose and said; –
– 'What little sense I once possessed
  Has quite gone out of my head!' –
And since that day he wanders still
By lake and forest, marsh and hill,
Singing – 'O somewhere, in valley or plain
'Might I find my Jumbly Girl again!
'For ever I'll seek by lake and shore
'Till I find my Jumbly Girl once more!'

  Playing a pipe with silvery squeaks,
  Since then his Jumbly Girl he seeks,
  And because by night he could not see,
  He gathered the bark of the Twangum Tree
    On the flowery plain that grows.
    And he wove him a wondrous Nose, –
  A Nose as strange as a Nose could be!
Of vast proportions and painted red,
And tied with cords to the back of his head.
    – In a hollow rounded space it ended
  With a luminous Lamp within suspended,
    All fenced about
    With a bandage stout
    To prevent the wind from blowing it out; –
  And with holes all round to send the light,
  In gleaming rays on the dismal night.

And now each night, and all night long,
Over those plains still roams the Dong;
And above the wail of the Chimp and Snipe

You may hear the squeak of his plaintive pipe
While ever he seeks, but seeks in vain
To meet with his Jumbly Girl again;
Lonely and wild – all night he goes, –
The Dong with a luminous Nose!
And all who watch at the midnight hour,
From Hall or Terrace, or lofty Tower,
Cry, as they trace the Meteor bright,
Moving along through the dreary night, –
  'This is the hour when forth he goes,
  'The Dong with a luminous Nose!
  'Yonder – over the plain he goes;
   'He goes!
   'He goes;
  'The Dong with a luminous Nose!'

IX
THE LONELY SHORE

THE QUANGLE WANGLE'S HAT

I

On the top of the Crumpetty Tree
   The Quangle Wangle sat,
But his face you could not see,
   On account of his Beaver Hat.
For his Hat was a hundred and two feet wide,
   With ribbons and bibbons on every side
And bells, and buttons, and loops, and lace,
   So that nobody ever could see the face
      Of the Quangle Wangle Quee.

II

The Quangle Wangle said
   To himself on the Crumpetty Tree, –
'Jam; and jelly; and bread;
   'Are the best food for me!
'But the longer I live on this Crumpetty Tree
'The plainer than ever it seems to me
'That very few people come this way
'And that life on the whole is far from gay!'
      Said the Quangle Wangle Quee.

But there came to the Crumpetty Tree,
   Mr and Mrs Canary;
And they said – 'Did you ever see
   'Any spot so charmingly airy?
'May we build a nest on your lovely Hat?
'Mr Quangle Wangle, grant us that!
'O please let us come and build a nest
'Of whatever material suits you best,
    'Mr Quangle Wangle Quee!'

IV

And besides, to the Crumpetty Tree
   Came the Stork, the Duck, and the Owl;
The Snail, and the Bumble-Bee,
   The Frog, and the Fimble Fowl;
(The Fimble Fowl, with a Corkscrew leg;)
And all of them said, – 'We humbly beg,
   'We may build our homes on your lovely Hat, –
   'Mr Quangle Wangle, grant us that!
    'Mr Quangle Wangle Quee!'

V

And the Golden Grouse came there,
   And the Pobble who has no toes, –
And the small Olympian bear, –
   And the Dong with a luminous nose.
And the Blue Baboon, who played the flute, –
And the Orient Calf from the Land of Tute, –
And the Attery Squash, and the Bisky Bat, –
All came and built on the lovely Hat
   Of the Quangle Wangle Quee.

And the Quangle Wangle said
   To himself on the Crumpetty Tree, –
'When all these creatures move
   'What a wonderful noise there'll be!'
And at night by the light of the Mulberry moon
They danced to the Flute of the Blue Baboon,
On the broad green leaves of the Crumpetty Tree,
And all were as happy as happy could be,
   With the Quangle Wangle Quee.

THE COURTSHIP OF THE YONGHY-BONGHY-BÒ

I

On the Coast of Coromandel
Where the early pumpkins blow,
In the middle of the woods
   Lived the Yonghy-Bonghy-Bò.
Two old chairs, and half a candle, –
One old jug without a handle, –
    These were all his worldly goods:
    In the middle of the woods,
    These were all the worldly goods,
   Of the Yonghy-Bonghy-Bò,
   Of the Yonghy-Bonghy-Bò.

II

Once, among the Bong-trees walking
   Where the early pumpkins blow,
    To a little heap of stones

180

Came the Yonghy-Bonghy-Bò.
There he heard a Lady talking,
To some milk-white Hens of Dorking, —
    ' 'Tis the Lady Jingly Jones!
    'On that little heap of stones
    'Sits the Lady Jingly Jones!'
Said the Yonghy-Bonghy-Bò,
Said the Yonghy-Bonghy-Bò.

III

'Lady Jingly! Lady Jingly!
  'Sitting where the pumpkins blow,
    'Will you come and be my wife!'
Said the Yonghy-Bonghy-Bò.
'I am tired of living singly, —
'On this coast so wild and shingly, —
    'I'm a-weary of my life:
    'If you'll come and be my wife,
    'Quite serene would be my life!' —
Said the Yonghy-Bonghy-Bò,
Said the Yonghy-Bonghy-Bò.

IV

'On this Coast of Coromandel,
  'Shrimps and watercresses grow,
    'Prawns are plentiful and cheap,'
Said the Yonghy-Bonghy-Bò.
'You shall have my chairs and candle,
'And my jug without a handle! —
    'Gaze upon the rolling deep
    ('Fish is plentiful and cheap)
    'As the sea, my love is deep!'
Said the Yonghy-Bonghy-Bò,
Said the Yonghy-Bonghy-Bò.

V

Lady Jingly answered sadly,
  And her tears began to flow, –
    'Your proposal comes too late,
    'Mr Yonghy-Bonghy-Bò!
'I would be your wife most gladly!'
(Here she twirled her fingers madly,)
      'But in England I've a mate!
      'Yes! you've asked me far too late,
      'For in England I've a mate,
    'Mr Yonghy-Bonghy-Bò!
    'Mr Yonghy-Bonghy-Bò!'

VI

'Mr Jones – (his name is Handel, –
  'Handel Jones, Esquire, & Co.)
    'Dorking fowls delights to send,
    'Mr Yonghy-Bonghy-Bò!
'Keep, oh! keep your chairs and candle,
And your jug without a handle, –
      'I can merely be your friend!
      '– Should my Jones more Dorkings send,
      'I will give you three, my friend!
    'Mr Yonghy-Bonghy-Bò!
    'Mr Yonghy-Bonghy-Bò!'

VII

'Though you've such a tiny body,
  'And your head so large doth grow, –
    'Though your hat may blow away,
    'Mr Yonghy-Bonghy-Bò!
'Though you're such a Hoddy Doddy –
'Yet I wish that I could modi-

'fy the words I needs must say!
'Will you please to go away?
'That is all I have to say –
'Mr Yonghy-Bonghy-Bò!
'Mr Yonghy-Bonghy-Bò!'

VIII

Down the slippery slopes of Myrtle,
　Where the early pumpkins blow,
　　To the calm and silent sea
　Fled the Yonghy-Bonghy-Bò.
There, beyond the Bay of Gurtle,
Lay a large and lively Turtle; –
　　'You're the Cove,' he said, 'for me;
　　'On your back beyond the sea,
　　'Turtle, you shall carry me!'
　Said the Yonghy-Bonghy-Bò,
　Said the Yonghy-Bonghy-Bò.

IX

Through the silent-roaring ocean
  Did the Turtle swiftly go;
    Holding fast upon his shell
  Rode the Yonghy-Bonghy-Bò.
With a sad primæval motion
Towards the sunset isles of Boshen
    Still the Turtle bore him well.
    Holding fast upon his shell,
     'Lady Jingly Jones, farewell!'
  Sang the Yonghy-Bonghy-Bò,
  Sang the Yonghy-Bonghy-Bò.

X

From the Coast of Coromandel,
  Did that Lady never go;
    On that heap of stones she mourns
  For the Yonghy-Bonghy-Bò.
On that Coast of Coromandel,
In his jug without a handle
    Still she weeps, and daily moans;
    On that little heap of stones
    To her Dorking Hens she moans,
  For the Yonghy-Bonghy-Bò,
  For the Yonghy-Bonghy-Bò.

INCIDENTS IN THE LIFE OF MY UNCLE ARLY

I

O My agèd Uncle Arly!
Sitting on a heap of Barley
  Thro' the silent hours of night, –
Close beside a leafy thicket: –
On his nose there was a Cricket, –
In his hat a Railway-Ticket; –
  (But his shoes were far too tight.)

II

Long ago, in youth, he squander'd
All his goods away, and wander'd
  To the Tiniskoop-hills afar.
There on golden sunsets blazing,
Every evening found him gazing, –
Singing, – 'Orb! you're quite amazing!
  'How I wonder what you are!'

III

Like the ancient Medes and Persians,
Always by his own exertions
  He subsisted on those hills; –
Whiles, – by teaching children spelling, –
Or at times by merely yelling, –
Or at intervals by selling
  Propter's Nicodemus Pills.

Later, in his morning rambles
He perceived the moving brambles –
　　Something square and white disclose; –
'Twas a First-class Railway-Ticket;
But, on stooping down to pick it
Off the ground, – a pea-green Cricket
　　Settled on my uncle's Nose.

V

Never – never more, – oh! never,
Did that Cricket leave him ever, –
　　Dawn or evening, day or night; –
Clinging as a constant treasure, –
Chirping with a cheerious measure, –
Wholly to my uncle's pleasure, –
　　(Though his shoes were far too tight.)

VI

So for three-and-forty winters,
Till his shoes were worn to splinters,
　　All those hills he wander'd o'er, –
Sometimes silent; – sometimes yelling; –
Till he came to Borley-Melling,
Near his old ancestral dwelling; –
　　(But his shoes were far too tight.)

VII

On a little heap of Barley
Died my agèd uncle Arly,
　　And they buried him one night; –
Close beside the leafy thicket; –
There, – his hat and Railway-Ticket; –
There, – his ever-faithful Cricket; –
　　(But his shoes were far too tight.)

X

SOME INCIDENTS IN THE LIFE OF EDWARD LEAR

MR LEAR'S WURBL INWENTIONS
and
ENVOI

№ 1

Mr Lear a reading of ῥωδῖῶ ἐ CSPF. I letters
under his an olive tree.   April 4. 1871

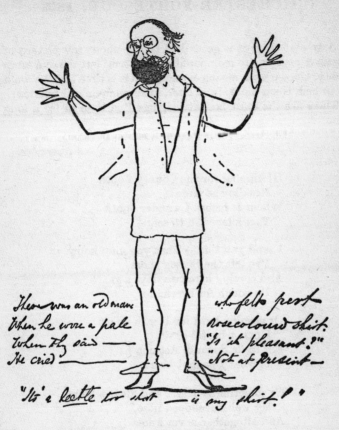

There was an old man who felt pert
 When he wore a pale rosecoloured shirt.
When they said – 'Is it pleasant?'
He cried – 'Not at present –
'It's a *leetle* too short – is my shirt!'

VERSES IN A LETTER TO HIS FRIEND
CHICHESTER FORTESCUE: 1859

O dear me! there is a good deal to say about my picture of Bassæ & many more mompophlious matters: but the dim lamp wanes: the dark sea moans & roars, and it is time that I should go to bed. Good-night. [and later, after removing to London]

These are the most bestest lodgings I've been in for a long time.

15, STRATFORD PLACE, OXFORD STREET,

4 November.

O! Mimber for the County Louth
   Residing at Ardee!
Whom I, before I wander South
   Partik'lar wish to see: –

I send you this. – That you may know
   I've left the Sussex shore,
And coming here two days ago
   Do cough for evermore.

Or gasping hard for breath do sit
   Upon a brutal chair,
For to lie down in Asthma fit
   Is what I cannot bear.

Or sometimes sneeze: and always blow
   My well-develloped nose.
And altogether never know
   No comfort nor repose.

All through next week I shall be here,
   To work as best I may,
On my last picture, which is near-
   -er finished every day.

But after the thirteenth – (that's Sunday)
   I must – if able – start
(Or on the Tuesday if not Monday,)
   For England's Northern part.

And thence I only come again
   Just to pack up and run
Somewhere where life may less be pain,
   And somewhere where there's sun.

So then I hope to hear your ways
   Are bent on English moves
For that I trust once more to gaze
   Upon the friend I loves.

(Alas! Blue Posts I shall not dare
   To visit ere I go –
Being compulsed to take such care
   Of all the winds as blow.)

But if you are not coming now
   Just write a line to say so –
And I shall still consider how
   Ajoskyboskybayso.

No more my pen: no more my ink:
   No more my rhyme is clear.
So I shall leave off here I think –
   Yours ever,

                  EDWARD LEAR.

FULMINATIONS AFTER A PAINTING
EXPEDITION TO MOUNT ATHOS

In a letter to Chichester Fortescue: 1856

So I said, I'll go to Mt Athos: (I should have gone to M. Negro
with A. Seymour had I not missed the steamer). And off I set on
Aug. 7th taking my servant, canteen, bed & lots of paper &
Quinine Pills. F. Lushington saw me as far as φιλαθες, but then I
fell down a high flight of (19) stone stairs & damaged my back
sadly. I thought I was lame for life, but after 4 days on a mat
tress, I got on pillows & a horse, & went over to Yannina & to
Pindus, & (in great pain) to Larissa, & finally to Saloniki. There
getting better I went slick into Tó "Αγιος "Θρος or the Holy
Mountain, altogether the most surprising thing I have seen in
my travels, perhaps, barring Egypt. It is a peninsular mountain
about 2000ft. high & 50 miles long ending in a vast crag, near
7000 feet high, this being Athos. All but this bare crag is one
mass of vast forest, beech, chestnut, oak, & ilex, and all round
the cliffs and crags by the sea are 20 great and ancient monistir-
ries, not to speak of 6 or 700 little 'uns above and below and
around. These convents are inhabited by, altogether perhaps, 6
or 7000 monx, & as you may have heard, no female creature
exists in all the peninsula: – there are nothing but mules,
tomcats, & cocks allowed. This is literally true.

Well, I had a great deal of suffering in this Athos, for my good
man Giorgio caught the fever, & nearly died, & when he grew
better I caught it, but not so badly. However I persisted &
persisted & finally I got drawings of every one of the 20 big
monasteries, so that such a valuable collection is hardly to be
found. Add to this, constant walking – 8 or 10 hours a day –
made me very strong, & the necessity I was under of acting
decidedly in some cases, called out a lot of energy I had for-
gotten ever to have possessed. The worst was the food & the
filth, which were uneasy to bear. But however wondrous and
picturesque the exterior & interior of the monasteries, & however
abundantly & exquisitely glorious & stupendous the scenery

of the mountain, I would not go again to the *"Aγιος "Oρος*, for any money, so gloomy, so shockingly unnatural, so lonely, so lying, so unatonably odious seems to me all the atmosphere of such monkery. That half of our species which it is natural to every man to cherish & love best, ignored, prohibited and abhorred – all life spent in everlasting repetition of monotonous prayers, no sympathy with ones fellow-beans of any nation, class or age. The name of Christ on every garment and at every tongue's end, but his maxims trodden under foot. God's world and will turned upside down, maimed, & caricatured: – if this I say be Xtianity let Xtianity be rooted out as soon as possible. More pleasing in the sight of the Almighty I really believe, & more like what Jesus Christ intended man to become, is an honest Turk with 6 wives, or a Jew working hard to feed his little old clo' babbies, than these muttering, miserable, mutton-hating, man-avoiding, misogynic, morose, & merriment-marring, monotoning, many-mule-making, mocking, mournful, minced-fish & marmalade masticating Monx. Poor old pigs!

A week or two later Edward Lear wrote this sequel: –

Here my boy! give me your eternal thanks for what I am going to suggest to you as a parliamentary motion, to be brought out & spoken on by yourself, to the ultimate benefit of society & to your own post-perpetual glorification. As soon as Parliament meets, move that all Sidney Herbert's distressed needle-women be sent out at once to Mount Athos! By this dodge all the 5000 monks young and old will be vanquished: – distressed needle-babies will ultimately awake the echoes of ancient Acte, & the whole fabric of monkery, not to say of the Greek church will fall down crash & for ever. N.B. Let the needle-women be all landed at once, 4000 at least, on the South-east side of the peninsula & make a rush for the nearest monastery, that subdued, all the rest will speedily follow.

A PESSIMISTIC CONVERSATION

Setting out for India in 1873, Edward Lear met a German Pessimist who sought to advise him on the spectacles he should wear. The following conversation took place: –

G.P. You vear spegtacles alvays?

E.L. Yes.

G.P. They vill all grack in India; von pair no use.

E.L. But I have many pairs.

G.P. How many?

E.L. Twenty or thirty.

G.P. No good. They vill all grack. You should have got of silver.

E.L. But I have several of silver. ,

G.P. Dat is no use; they vill rust; you might got gold.

E.L. But I have some of gold.

G.P. Dat is more vorse; gold is alvays stealing.

End of conversation.

FOUR STRANGE LETTERS TO HIS FRIEND EVELYN BARING

1. deerbaringiphowndacuppelloffotografsthismawningwitchi-
    sendjootothereiswunofeechsortsoyookankeepbothifyooliketo-
    doosoanwenyoohaveabettawunofyourselfletmehavit

                                                yossin seerly,

2.

Dear Baring,

Disgusticle to say, I must beg you to thank His Excellency from me, and to relate that I cannot come. I was engaged to dine with the DeVere's, but am too unwell with awful cold in the head and eyes to go out at all.

I have sent for two large tablecloths to blow my nose on, having already used up all my handkerchiefs. And altogether I am so unfit for company that I propose getting into a bag and being hung up to a bough of a tree till this tyranny is overpast. Please give the serming I send to His Excellency.

Yours sincerely,
Edward Lear

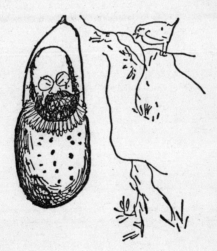

3.

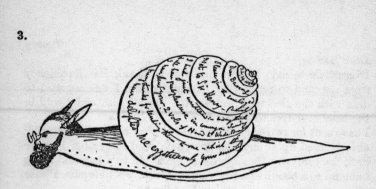

4

Feb.

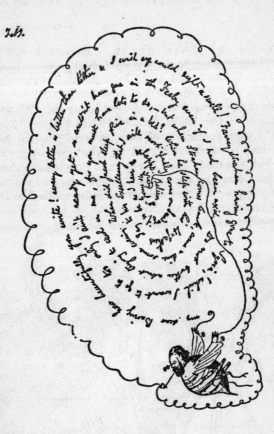

A STORY OF THE BOOK OF NONSENSE

[told in a letter to his friend Lady Waldegrave, 1866]

15, STRATFORD PLACE, OXFORD ST.
W.
17 October 1866.

MY DEAR LADY WALDEGRAVE, – It is orfle cold here, and I don't know what to do. I think I shall go to Jibberolter, passing through Spain, and doing Portigle later. After all one isn't a potato – to remain always in one place.

A few days ago in a railway as I went to my sister's a gentleman explained to two ladies, (whose children had my 'Book of Nonsense',) that thousands of families were grateful to the author (which in silence I agreed to) who was not generally known – but was really Lord Derby: and now came a showing forth, which cleared up at once to my mind why that statement has already appeared in several papers. Edward Earl of Derby (said the Gentleman) did not choose to publish the book openly,

but dedicated it as you see to his relations, and now if you will transpose the letters LEAR you will read simply EDWARD EARL. – Says I, joining spontanious in the conversation – 'That is quite a mistake: I have reason to know that Edward Lear the painter and author wrote and illustrated the whole book.' 'And I,' says the Gentleman, says he – 'have good reason to know Sir, that you are wholly mistaken. *There is no such a person* as Edward Lear.' 'But,' says I, 'there *is* – and I am the man – and I wrote the book!' Whereon all the party burst out laughing and evidently thought me mad or telling fibs. So I took off my hat and showed it all round, with Edward Lear and the address in large letters – also one of my cards, and a pocket handkerchief: on which amazement devoured those benighted individuals and I left them to gnash their teeth in trouble and tumult.

Believe me, Dear Lady Waldegrave,
Yours sincerely,
EDWARD LEAR

Foss Couchant

Foss, a untin.

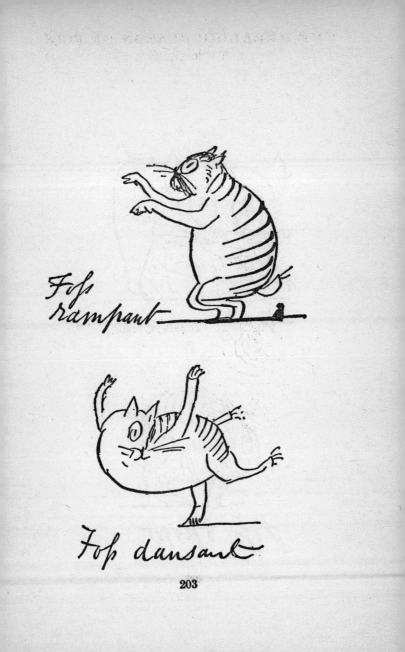

Fch
rampant

Fch dansant

Foss, regardant

Foss Pprpr.

Foss, Passant

MR LEAR'S WURBL INWENTIONS
a little dictionary

ABOUNDIGLE: a form of *abunjiant*. Thus: 'Letters have been aboundigle'; or 'The Russians have spies abunjiant everywhere'.

ABSALOMLY: 'It is absalomly necessary for me to have some subject to grind upon'.

ABSQUATULATE: to stand up. ' "God Save the Queen" was called for and we all absquatulated'.

ABSQUOXIOUSLY: a term of effusive greeting, as in 'Yours absquoxiously and full of blomphious and umpsidixious congratulations'.

ABUNJIANT: see *aboundigle*

AJOO: farewell

AMBLONGUS: picked fresh and boiled in a small pipkin they form the chief ingredient of 'amblongus pie'. See p. 129

ASSMA: complaint of nonsense poets, brought on especially by *squondangerlous* conditions.

BEFIZZLED: Mentone 'too shut in and befizzled a place for me'.

BESPRINGLED: esp. of stars. See p. 145

BLOMPHIOUS: see *absquoxiously*

BOSHBLOBBERBOSH: particularly foolish foolishness.

BUNDY: the day immediately preceding *Toosdy* and *Weddlesday*. Its first half sometimes referred to as 'Bunday Bording'

BUPLISHER: a person with whom negrotiations take place for buplishing books.

BUZZIM: 'Think of laying your head, my head I mean, after long, long hours of weary outline drawing – not on the hard bolster of the tent bed, but on an intelligent female's buzzim!' Thus: *buzzimless* and *unbuzzomed*. See also *fewcher* and *epopsimate*

CARRYVAN: a small *pamteggnikon*

CLIPFOMBIOUS: of landscape: 'the views over the harbour are of the most clipfombious and ompsiquillious nature'.

CONFLATULATION: 'I must tell you with a feeling of pride and conflatulation that I have made much progress in Greek'.

COTTS: Mary Squeen of.

COUGHY: 'From 8 to 9 I breakfast audibly in the public coughy-room'.

CRUMBOBBLIOUS: a sauce used on 'crumbobblious cutlets'. See p. 130

DARMONY: see *pease*

DIMBEMISTED: 'I am very dimbemisted-cloudybesquashed as to plans'.

DOLOMPHIOUS: of ducks. See p. 106

DREKKLY: 'If you wish me to call on him, I will do so drekkly'.

EGGZIBISSION: especially of *pigchurs*. Similarly: 'eggspire', 'eggstrax', and 'eggzi stens'.

EPISSEL: 'I must go to bed & finish this blessed epissel tomorrow'.

EPOPSIMATE: as in 'to epopsimate the fangropunxious feelings of my *buzzim*'.

FAX: see *fuliginous* and *granulously*

FEWCHER: 'Whether I shall come to England next year or knot is as yet idden in the mists of the fewcher'. May also have a *buzzim*, or may serve in such compounds as 'fewcherome'.

FLUMPING: of pilgrims in the Ganges ('squash'); and of pelicans, See p. 67

FIZZICLE: of maladies such as *assma* and *roomatizim*. Similarly 'fizziognomy',

FIZZGIGGIOUS: of fish. See p. 108

42de: a 4mula also used in addressing the Rt. Hon. Chichester 40scue Esq., friend of the poet (known in Latin as Excelscue, i.e. XLscue).

FULIGINOUS: of steamers (fuliginous and flea-full); and *fax* (fuliginous and filthy).

GALLOOBIOUS: of neatly dressed and genteel sparrows.

GIRAFFINOS: found in zoos with 'hippopotamice'. See also *squeegles*

GLUMY: 'The people nearly all dress in black, which makes a glumy appierance'.

GNOAT: 'This is a nextra gnoat – along of a nun4seen stircumsance'.

GRANULOUSLY: 'Witch *fax* I only came at granulously as it were – grain by grain, as the pigeon said when he picked up the bushel of corn slowly'.

GRISOGORIOUS: of scenery, a contrast to *clipfombious*

GROMFIBBEROUS: see *pomskizillious*

HART: vorx of.

INSTITOOTION: frequently 'carrotable'.

JOON: arrives two months before Orgst, which itself precedes Ortum.

JUMSIBOJIGGLEQUACK: 'Whereby I shall go to Sardinia or India or Jumsibojigglequack this next winter as ever is'.

LUMPSHON: 'Accept my gratitudes – and may you meet with beattitudes – whereon I'll write no more platitudes – but will go to lumpshon with a cleary conscience'.

MELOOBIOUS: of the sound of the rolling river

MUCILAGINOUS: of monx (see p. 194); of monotony; of minds; of melodious sounds; and of monkeys ('On the whole, as the morbid and mucilaginous monkey said when he climbed to the top of the Palm-tree and found no fruit there, one can't depend upon dates . . .')

MUMBIAN: a kind of melody. See p. 62

NARTIST: a person engaged in making vorx of *hart*

N.R.G.s: 'I could work no more till something called out my boddly & mentle N.R.G.s'.

OJOUS: hateful. 'If things get more ojous here, I must leave earlier'.

OMBLIFEROUS: 'There was a Young Person of Crete,
Whose toilette was far from complete
She dressed in a sack, spickle-speckled with black,
That ombliferous person of Crete.'

OMPSIQUILLIOUS: see *clipfombious*

OSSIFERS: leading participants in 'milingtary specktickles'.

OZBERVATIONS: esp in correspondence: 'The only ozbervation I shall permit myself about its appearance, is that your Lordship's writing gets more of the curly-burly roly-poly nature than is consistent with elegant and legible grammatography'.

PAMTEGGNIKON: a large *carryvan*

PEASE: as in 'pease an darmony'.

PHILOPOBOSTROGOTROBBICLE: an important question involving cabinet puddings.

PHITS: usually of coffin.

PHOGGS: or, when serious, 'thikphoggs'.

PIGCHURS: usually done by a *nartist* and placed in an *eggzibission*.

PIPKINIOUS: 'I drink very admirable small beer plenteously from pewter pipkinious pots'.

PLUMDOMPHIOUS: of the walking Co-operative Cauliflower. See p. 148

POAST: breakfast nourishment, usually eaten in 'tieces'.

POBBLESQUATTLES: an exclamation, as in:
'O pumpkins! O periwinkles!
O pobblesquattles! how him rain!'

POLITIX: an activity engaged in by Polly Titians

POMSIDILLIOUS: rather like *triumphiliginous*; not to be confused with:

POMSKIZILLIOUS: 'The Coast Scenery may truly be called pomskizillious and gromphibberous, being as no words can describe its magnificence'.

PONGDOMPHIOUS: an expression of gloom: 'I must say that life becomes werry werry pongdomphious'.

PUMPTILIOUSLY: 'I want to leave everything here in a pumptiliously exactual condition'.

PURPLEDICULAR: of crags. See pp. 95-6

QUAPSFILLIOUS: of delicate questions.

REM: as in 'Piers of the Rem'.

ROOMATIZIM: as *assma*; also 'roomattics'.

RUNCIBLE: of spoons, cats, geese, walls, ravens and hats. See pp. 66, 86, 98, 120 and 213.

SCRIBBLEBIBBLE: a minor *epissel*

SCROOBIOUS: 'You ax about my plans: they are still at a scroobious, dubious doubtfulness'. See also pp. 49, 121 and 143.

SKLIMJIMFIOUSNESS: of situations, usually improving ones.

SKLOMBIONBIOUSLY: of situations, usually satisfactory.

SKRIGGLE: to manage (but only just).

SKROGFRODIOUS: as in the 'bilious and skrogfrodious temperament' of a *nartist*

SLOBACIOUS: of moonshine. See p. 145

SNEEZIGRAPH: '.... vainly seeking a method by which I can multiply my 200 designs by photograph or autograph, or sneezigraph or any other graph'.

SOPHISTICLE: see *stereopyptic*

SPLOMBONGLIFIED: of religious attitudes.

SPONGETANEOUSLY: of crickets coming suddenly to life in the cellar.

SQUIGGS: an exclamation of disgust, as in 'Squiggs. Beetles. Bother. Bullfrogs. Buttercups. Let us change the subject.'

SQUEEGLES: to be seen at the zoo, along with vulchers, eagles, seagles and beagles.

SQUONDANGERLOUS: of weather: 'the day highly beastly and squondangerlous'.

STEREOPYPTIC: 'the stereopyptic and sophisticle steamer'.

STIRCUMSANCE: see *gnoat*

TOOSDY: see *Bundy*

TRIUMPHILIGINOUS: rather like *pomsidillious*

UNPHORTSCHNIT: a condition in which a *nartist* may often find himself.

WEDDLESDAY: see *Bundy*

WEEVIL: as in: 'sufficient unto the day is the weevil thereof'.

WHIZZLEPOPPS: 'I am absolutely uncertain when I leave – or what to do – or why: or which: or whizzlepopps . . .'

YOTT: as opposed to stereopyptic and sophisticle steamer.

ENVOI: HOW PLEASANT TO KNOW MR LEAR

How pleasant to know Mr Lear!
  Who has written such volumes of stuff!
Some think him ill-tempered and queer,
  But a few think him pleasant enough.

His mind is concrete and fastidious,
  His nose is remarkably big;
His visage is more or less hideous,
  His beard it resembles a wig.

He has ears, and two eyes, and ten fingers,
  Leastways if you reckon two thumbs;
Long ago he was one of the singers,
  But now he is one of the dumbs.

He sits in a beautiful parlour,
  With hundreds of books on the wall;
He drinks a great deal of Marsala,
  But never gets tipsy at all.

He has many friends, laymen and clerical;
  Old Foss is the name of his cat;
His body is perfectly spherical,
  He weareth a runcible hat.

When he walks in a waterproof white,
  The children run after him so!
Calling out, 'He's come out in his night-
  Gown, that crazy old Englishman, oh!'

He weeps by the side of the ocean,
  He weeps on the top of the hill;
He purchases pancakes and lotion,
  And chocolate shrimps from the mill.

He reads but he cannot speak Spanish,
  He cannot abide ginger-beer:
Ere the days of his pilgrimage vanish,
  How pleasant to know Mr Lear!

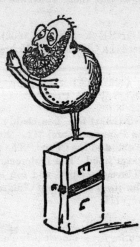

RECEIPT FOR SAUCES

THE ingredients for *A Book of Bosh* have come from a variety of books and documents. Among those which are out of copyright we have used:

A BOOK OF NONSENSE (3rd edition, 1862) for those limericks in Parts I and VII where the Old Men and Young Persons are given capital letters;

JOURNAL OF A LANDSCAPE PAINTER IN CORSICA (1868) for the Moral Fable in Part VI;

NONSENSE SONGS (1871) for 'The Daddy Long-legs and the Fly', 'The Owl and the Pussy-cat', and 'The Duck and the Kangaroo' in Part II; 'The Table and the Chair', 'The Broom, the Shovel, the Poker and the Tongs', and 'The Nutcrackers and the Sugar-tongs' in Part III; 'Three Receipts' and ten items of 'Nonsense Botany' in Part V; 'The Story of the Four Children' in Part VI; and 'The Jumblies' in Part VIII;

MORE NONSENSE (1872) for the 'Twenty-Six Nonsense Rhymes' in Part V; and for those limericks in Parts I and VII where the old men and young persons do not have capital letters (except for the four noted in the Acknowledgements below);

LAUGHABLE LYRICS (1877) for 'The Pelican Chorus' in Part II; the First Part of 'Mr and Mrs Discobbolos' in Part III; 'the New Vestments', 'The Two Old Bachelors' and 'The Pobble' in Part IV; two items from 'Nonsense Botany' in Part V; 'The Dong' in Part VIII; and 'The Quangle Wangle's Hat' and 'The Courtship of the Yonghy-Bonghy-Bò' in Part IX;

NONSENSE SONGS (1895) for the Second Part of 'Mr and Mrs Discobbolos' in Part III; 'Incidents in the Life of my Uncle Arly' in Part IX; the 'Heraldic Blazons' in Part X; and the Envoi;

THE LETTERS OF EDWARD LEAR (1907) for the title drawings, etc., to Parts II, V and X (ωρ); 'The Shortness of Shirts', the 'Verses', the 'Fulminations' and the 'self-portraits' in Part X;

THE LATER LETTERS OF EDWARD LEAR (1911) for the title drawings, etc., to Parts VI, IX and Acknowledgements; and the 'Story of the Book of Nonsense' in Part X;

QUEERY LEARY NONSENSE (1911) for the title-page drawing; 'Mrs Jaypher', 'Dingle Bank', 'An Epitaph' and 'The Last of Mrs Jaypher' in Part IV; the letters to Evelyn Baring in Part X, and the final drawing in the book.

ACKNOWLEDGEMENTS

For permission to use material still in copyright we are grateful to:

THE HARVARD COLLEGE LIBRARY for the limericks in Part I on the old persons of Harrow and Bradley, and the old men of Kildare and New York, from W. Osgood Field's *Edward Lear on my Shelves* (1933). The title drawing for Part IV, which was the basis for the cover design for *Laughable Lyrics* is also taken from this book;

H. P. Kraus for the drawing of the Sick Man of Tobago on page 8;

JOHN MURRAY (PUBLISHERS) LTD for the botanical pictures on page 10; the procession on page 12; and the drawing on page 153 from *Teapots and Quails* (1953); and the drawing on page 82; and the 'Pessimistic Conversation' in Part X from *Edward Lear* by Angus Davidson (1938);

THE PIERPONT MORGAN LIBRARY for the title-drawing for Part III, and the drawing and text for the title to Part VII;

THE TENNYSON RESEARCH CENTRE, LINCOLN, for the letter on page 82 found, like the immediately preceding item, in *Edward Lear; the life of a wanderer* by Vivien Noakes (1968). This letter is published by courtesy of Lord Tennyson and Lincolnshire Library Service.

WUTHERING HEIGHTS
Emily Brontë

One of the great romantic novels of all time, *Wuthering Heights* is set against the stark and haunting Yorkshire moors and tells the tragic love story of Heathcliff and Catherine.

ENGLISH FAIRY TALES
Joseph Jacobs

This anthology of traditional stories is a delightful combination of old favourites and little-known stories, collected by the scholar and story-teller Joseph Jacobs at the end of the nineteenth century. There are classics such as Jack and the Beanstalk, Tom Thumb and The Story of the Three Bears, as well as the less familiar The Laidly Worm of Spindleston Heugh and Mr Miacca. A classic collection to be enjoyed over and over again.

WELSH LEGENDS AND FOLK TALES
Gwyn Jones

Heroic deeds and high adventure abound in this rich collection of legends and folk tales from Wales. There's the story of Lleu and the bride made of flowers because of a mother's curse, the tale of the giant Rhitta and his strange obsession with collecting beards, and the classic love story of Trystan and Esyllt, among many others, all beautifully retold.

HANS ANDERSEN'S FAIRY TALES

translated by Naomi Lewis

A marvellous collection of fairy tales from Hans Andersen, chosen and newly translated by the eminent writer and critic Naomi Lewis. All the best-known and most-loved stories, Thumbelina, The Snow Queen, The Emperor's New Clothes, are included as well as the less familiar, The Goblin at the Grocer's and Dance, Dolly, Dance. Hans Andersen's timeless tales have been delighting generations of readers for over 150 years – no child should be without them.

KING ARTHUR AND HIS KNIGHTS OF THE ROUND TABLE

Roger Lancelyn Green

The immortal tales from the Court of King Arthur are tales about good overcoming evil, full of mystery, enchantment and chivalry. These stories about Merlin, King Arthur, Queen Guinevere and the Knights of the Round Table have been told for hundreds of years but are retold here with freshness, vitality and dignity. From the sword in the stone and the coming of King Arthur, the forging of Excalibur and the making of the Round Table, to the quest for the Holy Grail and Arthur's last battle, these age-old stories are as exciting as they were when they were first told.

FRANKENSTEIN

Mary Shelley

The fable of the scientist who creates a man-monster, and of the terrible events which follow, is one of the best-known horror stories ever. From the moment that Frankenstein's creation comes alive, the gripping story that unfolds with its murders and terrors is one that fills the reader with horror and trepidation – and a determination and compulsion to read on.

PINOCCHIO
Carlo Collodi

When the old wood-carver Gepetto decides to make a wonderful puppet who can dance and turn somersaults, he has no idea of the trouble in store. For as the puppet takes shape, it gradually comes to life, learning to talk and play pranks, providing a constant source of exasperation and delight. This translation is by E. Harden.

THE MAGIC WORLD
E. Nesbit

There's a whole world of magic waiting to enchant you when you read these stories. There's a cruel and mischievous boy who is taught a lesson he will never forget by his own pet cat, and another cat made of porcelain which saves the family heritage. A girl sent upstairs in disgrace is suddenly whisked off to the world of her dreams, and two boys make their fortunes by using a magical telescope: and many more tales to transport you to the world of the imagination.

THE ROSE AND THE RING
W. M. Thackeray

Fairy-tale, humour, fantasy and slapstick intermingle in this delightful and ingenious 'fireside pantomime' by the author of *Vanity Fair*. There's the hall porter who is turned into a door knocker for twenty years; rivalry between usurping scoundrels and rightful heirs; and four princes and princesses falling in and out of love with each other all because of the Fairy Blackstick's two magical presents: a rose and a ring.

LASSIE COME-HOME
Eric Knight

Lassie, the prize dog of a cottager's household, is sold to a wealthy family when hard times befall her owners. Taken hundreds of miles away, she does what many collies have done before her: she starts for home so that she can be faithful to a duty – that of meeting a boy by a schoolhouse gate. This classic dog story was made into a famous film and also gave rise to numerous later films and television dramas.

ALADDIN AND OTHER TALES FROM THE ARABIAN NIGHTS
Retold by N. J. Dawood

A poor ragamuffin finds an old lamp which makes his fortune, a fisherman becomes rich by casting his nets in an enchanted lake and a prince disappears on a flying horse! These tales of powerful kings and princes, magical genies and wicked magicians full of trickery were the daily entertainment of everyday people over a thousand years ago, and are retold here directly from the original Arabic sources.

TWENTY THOUSAND LEAGUES UNDER THE SEA
Jules Verne

A glorious mission to rid the seas of a monstrous creature becomes a terrifying nightmare when Professor Aronnax, Conseil and the harpooner, Ned Land, are thrown overboard. For the frigate has struck bare metal: the huge marine animal which has haunted the waters is no living beast, but a spectacular man-made vessel, and the three men find themselves the helpless prisoners of Captain Nemo. But what marvels the ocean has in store – for the Professor at least, this voyage is one he would not have missed for the world!

GREAT EXPECTATIONS
Charles Dickens

When young Pip is accosted in the graveyard by Magwitch, an escaped convict, and forced to help him, he little knows that their lives are destined to cross in future years. Pip's upbringing with his kindly uncle Joe, his involvement with the crazy world of the eccentric Miss Haversham and her beautiful young ward, the icy Estella, and then a new life in London, are all part of this classic story of a boy discovering the reality of 'great expectations'.

JANE EYRE
Charlotte Brontë

As an orphan, Jane Eyre's childhood is far from happy. She endures the hatred of her aunt and cousins, but finally begins to find some pleasure as a teacher. When she becomes a governess working for Mr Rochester, Jane hopes she might at last have found love and kindness, but are events to prove her wrong once more?

An enthralling story about love and betrayal, *Jane Eyre* is one of the most unforgettable of English novels.

KINGS AND QUEENS
poems by Eleanor and Herbert Farjeon

A delightful collection of poems – with witty and original illustrations by Robin Jacques – about all forty-one English Kings and Queens since William I. And there's no doubt as to who were the heroes and who were the villains: as Herbert Farjeon said, 'the Bad Kings are bad and the Good Kings are good, just as they used to be when we were children.' History has never been such fun!

SELECTED CAUTIONARY VERSES
Hilaire Belloc

Enjoy the exploits of Jim, who ran away from his nurse and was eaten by a lion; Matilda, Godolphin Horne and many more characters; each of these poems presents a hero or heroine with a very naughty habit. The naughtier they are, the worse the punishment – so there could be some lessons to be learnt!

HORNBLOWER GOES TO SEA
C. S. Forester

The dramatic sea-battles and adventures Hornblower faces take him from being a quiet yet strangely impressive young man, newly commissioned into Nelson's navy, to an intrepid commander on the high seas, making his mark as one of the most formidable officers ever to set sail.

VICE VERSA
F. Anstey

On an unforgettable Black Monday in January 1881, Paul Bultitude Esq. and his son Dick find themselves in an extra-ordinary situation: father is now son, and son father! The ensuing months can only be described as absolute mayhem.

ALLAN QUATERMAIN
H. Rider Haggard

The sequel to *King Solomon's Mines*, this magnificent adventure story tells of three men and their guide Umslopogaas, who trek into the remote interior of Africa in search of a lost white race. Through unknown territories their perilous journey finally takes them to Zu-Vendis, a kingdom ruled by the beautiful twin sisters Nyleptha and Sorais.

MR MIDSHIPMAN EASY
Captain Marryat

Little does Jack Easy realize when he joins the Royal Navy that he is entering a service in which equality could never for a moment exist. Life on the high seas is not all swashbuckling adventure and the wild ideas of Jack's ardent youth are soon put to the test. This rollicking, comic yarn offers a lighthearted view of life in the Royal Navy, and, more seriously, a dig at Jack's egalitarian philosophizing.

THE GREAT ADVENTURES OF SHERLOCK HOLMES
Sir Arthur Conan Doyle

No case is too challenging, no mystery too mysterious, no crime too serious for the Victorian super-sleuth, Sherlock Holmes, with his redoubtable assistant Dr Watson. The world's most famous private detective uses his unique powers of deduction and reasoning to solve the unsolvable, from the bizarre case of The Red-Headed League to the strange tale of The Solitary Cyclist and the extraordinary saga of The Engineer's Thumb.